The most comprehensive, illustrated history of the world

WORLD HISTORY

The Dark Ages
501– 1100

KING*f*ISHER

Kingfisher an imprint of Larousse plc
Elsley House, 24-30 Great Titchfield Street, London W1P 7AD

This edition published 1997
This edition Copyright © Larousse plc 1997
First published by Kingfisher 1992 as *The Kingfisher Illustrated History of the World*
Copyright © Larousse plc 1992, 1995

British Library Cataloguing-in-Publication Data
A catalogue record for this book is available from the British Library

ISBN 07534 0129 0

Typeset by Tradespools Ltd, Frome, Somerset
Printed in Italy

Contents

The Early Middle Ages

The years 501–1100 used to be called the Dark Ages because historians thought that civilization ended when the Roman empire fell. Many people now call these years the Early Middle Ages because they mark the start of the period separating ancient and modern history.

Although life after the Romans was different, the peoples who overran the western Roman empire were not all 'barbarians'. Many were farmers, skilled metal workers and ship-builders. The eastern Roman empire became the Byzantine empire. Under the Emperor Justinian, it even reconquered some land in North Africa, southern Spain and Italy. Much of this was later lost to the Arabs, who set up an Islamic empire.

The Chinese and the Arabs led the way in science and technology, medicine and astronomy. The Arabs adopted both the decimal system and the numbers 0 to 9 from India, and they learned how to make paper from the Chinese. This knowledge eventually passed to Europe.

Religion was spread through trade. Buddhism spread from China to Japan and other parts of South-East Asia. Many of the Vikings from Northern Europe, became Christians through trading with Christian countries. Islam was spread in a different way. As their empire grew, the Muslims converted the people they conquered. Muslim armies reached as far as France before being pushed back by new, stronger kingdoms who followed the teachings of the Christian Church.

▼ *A Viking village on the shores of a Norwegian fjord in about 800. Even the Vikings, thought to be a violent people, probably spent more of their time fishing and trading than fighting.*

The Americas

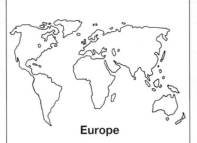

Europe

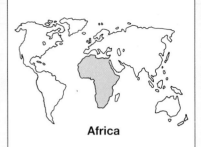

Africa

The Americas

c. **550** Huari, Moche and Nazca kingdoms flourish in Peru.

c. **600** In Central America Teotihuacán reaches the height of its power. In South America the cities of Tiahuanaco and Huari grow in size and importance.

c. **700** In North America the Temple Mound culture flourishes and the Anasazi people start to build pueblos.

c. **750** Both Teotihuacán and the Mayan states start to decline.

c. **800** The bow and arrow is first used in the Mississippi Valley.

c. **950** The Toltecs rise to power in Central America.

c. **985** The Vikings start to settle in Greenland

c. **1000** Chimú empire develops around Chan Chan in Northern Peru.

1003 The Viking Leif Ericsson travels to Newfoundland.

1100 The Anasazi culture reaches its greatest extent.

Europe

527 Justinian becomes Byzantine emperor and tries to revive the old Roman empire.

711 The Muslims invade Spain.

732 Charles Martel leads the Franks to victory over the Muslims at Poitiers, France.

771 Charlemagne comes to power in France. Under his rule, the feudal system starts to develop.

843 Charlemagne's empire is split into three parts.

911 The king of France gives Normandy to the Vikings.

955 Otto I of Germany defeats the Magyars at the battle of Lechfeld.

962 Otto I is crowned Holy Roman emperor.

1028 Canute conquers Norway. He is already king of Denmark and England.

1066 The Normans invade and conquer England.

1096 The First Crusade begins.

Africa

535 Justinian conquers North Africa and makes it part of the Byzantine empire.

569 In Sudan, the Nubian kingdom of Makuria is converted to Christianity.

639 The Arabs invade Egypt.

c. **690** In West Africa the state of Gao is founded near the Niger River.

c. **700** The whole of North Africa is now part of the Islamic empire. Arab traders start to cross the Sahara and trade with the peoples to the south of the desert. The kingdom of Ghana starts to grow rich on trade.

c. **900** The Tontsure state (modern Botswana) is established.

971 The world's first university is founded at Cairo in Egypt.

980 Arab merchants start to settle on the East African coast.

1000 The kingdom of Ghana is at its greatest.

1073 Ambassadors are sent to China from the East African port of Kilwa.

Near East

527 Emperor Justinian, sets out to conquer the Near East.
579 The Sassanian empire of Persia reaches its greatest extent.
622 The Hegira, when Muhammad flees to Medina. Start of the Muslim calendar.
632 Death of Muhammad; the Islamic empire starts to expand.
643 The Arabs conquer Persia and overthrow the Sassanian empire.

756 The Islamic empire starts to break up into separate countries.
762 Baghdad is founded by the Islamic leader al-Mansur.

An Islamic design from an 11th century Spanish ivory casket.

1096–99 The First Crusade reaches the Near East. Crusaders capture Jerusalem and set up a number of Christian states in the area.

Asia and the Far East

535 In India, the Gupta empire collapses.
581 The Sui dynasty is founded in China and reunites the country.
594 Buddhism becomes the official religion of Japan.
618 The Tang dynasty comes to power in China.
624 Buddhism becomes the official religion of China.
c. **775** The Kingdom of the Srijaya in Sumatra conquers the whole of the Malayan peninsula.

802 In Cambodia the Khmer dynasty establishes the kingdom of Angkor.
c. **811** The magnificent temple of Borobudur is built in Java.
868 The *Diamond Sutra* (the world's oldest surviving printed book) is printed in China.
960 The Song dynasty comes to power in China.

A Tang dynasty pottery bull

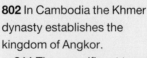

Australasia and Pacific

650 By this date all the Polynesian islands, except New Zealand, are colonized.

A giant head from Easter Island.

1000 The people of Easter Island start to carve huge stone statues. Polynesian peoples start to settle on the North Island of New Zealand.

The World

After the fall of the Roman empire new countries and peoples emerged in **Europe**. The lives of the people who lived in these countries were governed by the Christian Church and a rigid social system, later called feudalism.

Between Europe and the Far East there was a huge area containing many different people who all shared the same religion, **Islam**. Farther north, **Slav** countries such as Russia and Bulgaria were also forming.

China was still culturally and scientifically far in advance of the rest of the world. Its influence spread over **Asia**, and to Japan where there was a great flowering of the arts.

In **North America**, the first towns were being built and the Toltec civilization developed in Mexico. In **South America**, huge independent empires, such as the Huari empire, were forming.

Contact between the civilizations of the world was very limited. Only a few countries traded with each other. But Islam was gradually spread over the whole of **North Africa** through conquest and trade.

▶ The Vikings were great seafarers and travelled enormous distances in their flat-bottomed boats. They were the first Europeans to reach North America, landing there in about 1003. Later on they tried to establish settlements there.

NORTH AMERICA

Anasazi
MEXICO

Toltecs

SOUTH AMERICA

Huari empire

▲ The Toltecs were a warlike people who flourished in Mexico from 900 to 1100. Their temples were guarded by huge stone statues of warriors.

▲ The Anasazi people built pueblos (blocks of apartment-like houses). They performed elaborate ceremonies, asking for rain to water their desert surroundings.

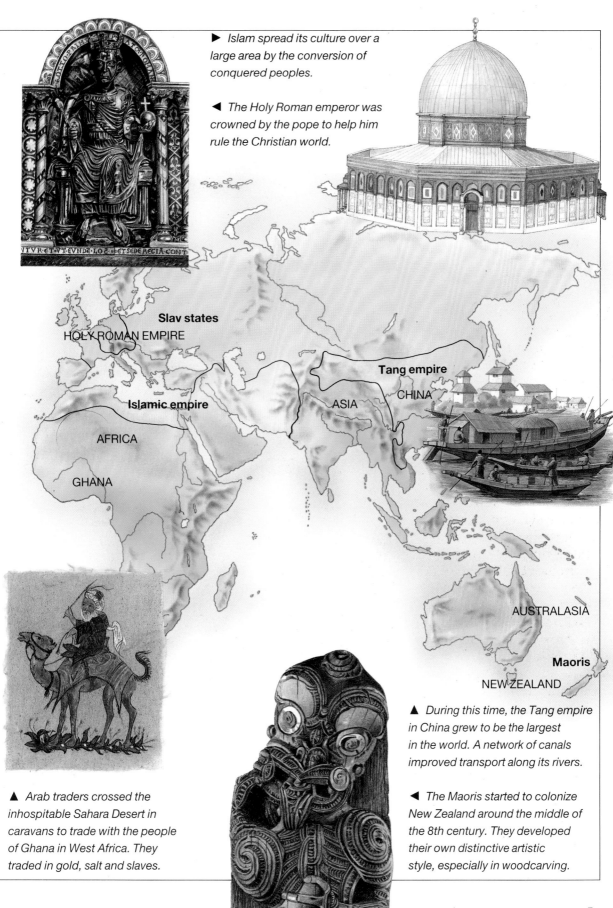

▶ Islam spread its culture over a large area by the conversion of conquered peoples.

◀ The Holy Roman emperor was crowned by the pope to help him rule the Christian world.

Slav states

HOLY ROMAN EMPIRE

Islamic empire

Tang empire

CHINA

ASIA

AFRICA

GHANA

AUSTRALASIA

Maoris

NEW ZEALAND

▲ During this time, the Tang empire in China grew to be the largest in the world. A network of canals improved transport along its rivers.

◀ The Maoris started to colonize New Zealand around the middle of the 8th century. They developed their own distinctive artistic style, especially in woodcarving.

▲ Arab traders crossed the inhospitable Sahara Desert in caravans to trade with the people of Ghana in West Africa. They traded in gold, salt and slaves.

c.501 Near East: Fighting starts between the Byzantine empire and Persia. Although they do not fight all the time, peace is not finally made until 642. Riders start to use stirrups; at first they are used for greater comfort when riding, later they are used in battle because they allow people to control their horses while fighting with swords, lances or bows and arrows.

503 Britain: The Britons under their legendary war leader Arthur defeat the Saxon invaders from Germany at the battle of Mount Badon.

505 Fighting between the Byzantine empire and Persia ends briefly.

Christian relics were greatly prized in the Byzantine empire. Elaborate caskets, decorated with enamelled pictures of Christ and the Apostles, were made to hold them.

507 France: Clovis, King of the Salian Franks from 481, leads his army to victory over the Visigoths near Poitiers. He is the grandson of Merovich and founder of the Merovingian dynasty. Clovis makes Paris the capital of his kingdom and introduces the Salic Law. This is concerned with both criminal and civil law. It remains important in later times since it forbids women to inherit land.

511 Clovis dies and his empire is divided between his four sons.

523 North Africa: Hilderic becomes king of the Vandals (to 530).

524 War flares up again between Byzantine empire and Persia. It lasts until 531.

525 Byzantine empire: Theodora, previously an actress, marries Prince Justinian, heir to the empire. During his rule, she pushes through laws which give women rights of property, inheritance and divorce.

The Byzantine Empire

Constantinople was the capital of the eastern half of the old Roman empire. It had been built on the Greek port of Byzantium and when the western Roman empire finally collapsed in 476, Constantinople became the capital of what is called the Byzantine empire.

At first, this empire only controlled a small amount of land around the Aegean Sea. Its emperors always hoped to defeat the barbarians so that they could reunite the former Roman empire. The peoples who attacked the empire also thought of its inhabitants as Romans.

During the Emperor Justinian's reign (527–565), under his general Belisarius, North Africa, Italy and southern Spain were reconquered and the empire was expanded to include all the eastern coast of the Mediterranean. But much of this land was lost soon after Justinian's death, by the end of the 6th century.

Constantinople, now called Istanbul, stood at the entrance to the Black Sea. It was on the land route between Europe and Asia and so it became an important trading centre. The empire produced

▼ *The empire reached its greatest extent under Justinian, but it was often threatened by its neighbours.*

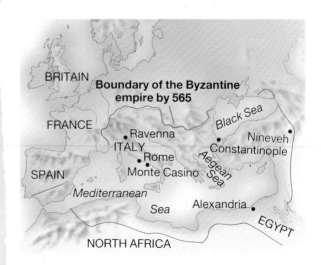

▲ *St Sophia, or the Church of Holy Wisdom, was built in Constantinople for Justinian between 532 and 537. It took over 10,000 people to construct it.*

gold, grain, olives, silk and wine, and these were traded for goods such as spices, precious stones, furs and ivory, from the Far East and from Africa.

The Byzantine empire was a centre of learning, where the knowledge of the Ancient Greeks was combined with the newer teachings of the Christian Church. It also had its own form of Christianity in the Orthodox Church. For centuries the greatest church in Christendom was St Sophia in Constantinople. The emperor was thought to be God's viceroy, or representative, on Earth and this idea later passed to the tsars of Russia.

JUSTINIAN AND THEODORA

Justinian *(below)* ruled the Byzantine empire with his wife, Empress Theodora. They believed their empire was the guardian of civilization and true religion. They also believed that laws should be something made by rulers, rather than something which was handed down as a custom. Under Justinian the old Roman law was reorganized and his ideas later spread back to western Europe.

Justinian's wife, Theodora helped him govern the empire. She had been an actress before her marriage and was considered very beautiful. Justinian relied on her for advice and support, and she changed laws to improve the lives of women and the poor.

▼ *The Byzantine empire was often attacked from both the land and from the sea. Its navy had a secret weapon called 'Greek fire'. It was a mixture of quick-lime, petroleum and sulphur which burst into flames once the quick-lime touched the water. Greek fire was very successful at keeping the enemy at bay and some people have called it the first modern weapon.*

Arts and Crafts

During this time much art was used for religious purposes. Byzantine churches were decorated with mosaics and with holy pictures called icons. In monasteries monks spent long hours copying out books by hand. To make the pages more attractive, they illuminated, or decorated, the capital letters. Muslims concentrated on calligraphy, or beautiful handwriting, and used words from the Koran to decorate buildings. The Germanic peoples were skilled metalworkers who made gold and silver jewellery. So did the Byzantines. The Chinese made pottery and porcelain, while others carved out patterns in wood and stone.

▲ This Byzantine mosaic is inside the church of San Vitale in Ravenna, Italy. Ravenna was briefly the capital of the Byzantine empire. It shows Theodora, wife of the Emperor Justinian presenting a gift for the church to two bishops.

▲ In the Song dynasty many of these pale green bowls, called celadons, were made for export from China. They were said to crack or change colour if poison was put into them.

▼ Maori woodcarvings, such as this totem pole, were cut out with stone axes. The patterns were then carved with stone points.

◀ Under Islamic law artists were not allowed to paint or draw pictures of human beings or animals. Instead they practised calligraphy, and decorated their texts with geometric designs or with flowing patterns of flowers and leaves. They often used gold leaf for the borders.

▼ Scribes used a lot of red lead called minium when illuminating capital letters. This led to small pictures being known as miniatures. They also used real gold and silver and inks in many colours.

▲ Alfred, King of Wessex, was a religious man who encouraged his people to go to church. This jewel may be one of a set which he had made. The originals had a pointer stuck in them and were used by the priest to keep his place when he was reading the Bible. The words around the edge of this one say 'Alfred had me made'.

WHEN IT HAPPENED

6th century Byzantine mosaics made from hundreds of pieces of coloured glass are used as decorations on the walls of churches.

625 The Anglian king Raedwald is buried in a ship at Sutton Hoo, Suffolk, with a hoard of treasure including gold jewellery set with garnets and a collection of silver bowls.

7th century The rapid growth of the Islamic empire spreads its own styles of art and writing to conquered countries.

9th century The Viking invaders are skilled metal, wood and stone workers. Their designs influence the people they settle amongst and are later used on churches.

900 The Chinese develop a hard, fine pottery, known as porcelain. It is made into cups, bowls and life-like figures.

10th century In Mexico the Toltecs carve stone warriors to guard their temples.

▼ Longships were such an important part of Viking life that their chiefs and queens were even buried with one. These ships reveal that the Vikings were skilled woodcarvers. Parts of the Oseberg ship, being built here, were decorated with detailed woodcarvings. Other Viking carvings include animal heads for frightening evil spirits, and engravings that tell stories.

Monasticism

From the earliest years of Christianity, some deeply religious people had chosen to live apart from everyone else, so that they could spend their time in prayer. They were known as hermits, and usually lived in remote places such as islands or deserts. In the 4th century, an Egyptian hermit, St Anthony of Thebes, brought several hermits together to form a community. This idea spread to other Christian countries and more communities of religious men, called monks, and women, called nuns, were established.

Some of these communities were

▲ St Benedict thought that the only way to escape evil in the world was to live a secluded and religious life.

▼ An early monastery was almost like a village. At its centre was a large church. This was surrounded by buildings where the monks ate, studied and worked. There were also kitchens, stables, and gardens for growing fruit, vegetables and medicinal herbs.

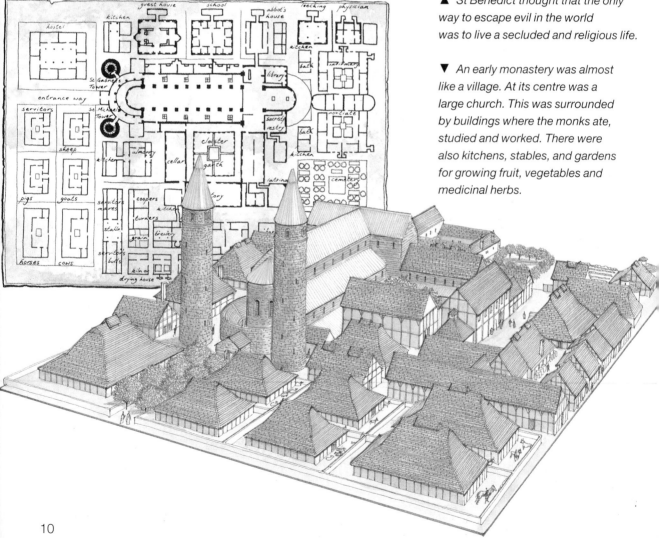

linked to each other by following the same 'rule'. This was a guide to how the community should live and was drawn up by a monastic leader. The most famous was the rule of St Benedict who founded the monastery of Monte Cassino in Italy in about 529. He said that a monk's life should be one of manual labour, as well as prayer and worship. Monks and nuns who followed his rule belonged to an Order, or group, known as Benedictines. They built communities all over Europe where they prayed and worked together as well as preaching to the local people.

By the 10th century other Orders had developed their own versions of the rule of St Benedict. One of these was the Cluniacs, who had their centre at Cluny in France. They spent most of their time in prayer and hired servants to do the daily chores. Another Order, the Cistercians, disagreed with this idea and divided their community into 'choir monks', who spent their time in prayer and administration, and 'lay brothers' who did the heavy work.

▲ Both nuns and monks were supposed to lead good, simple lives. As well as studying and praying, they had to grow food and look after the sick.

527 Justinian becomes ruler of the Byzantine empire (to 565).

529 Italy: The monastery of Monte Cassino, near Naples, is founded by St Benedict of Nursia. The monks who follow his rule are known as Benedictines. Although they lead a life of prayer and manual labour, the monks also provide almost all medical care and, by copying manuscripts, preserve much classical learning that would otherwise be lost.

A page from the Book of Durrow, made by Irish monks. Monks produced beautifully decorated books completely by hand. Scribes copied the text and artists decorated the borders and capital letters. One book may have been a lifetime's work.

529 Byzantine empire: Justinian starts to codify the laws which are based on the old Roman ones. They fill three volumes and it takes him until the end of his reign to complete them. (They go on to influence the law of nearly all European countries.) Justinian's empire also has its own form of Christianity, which exists today as the Eastern Orthodox Church.

530 North Africa: Gelimer becomes king of the Vandals (to 534).

533 The so-called 'Eternal Peace' treaty is signed between the Byzantine empire and Persia. It lasts for seven years.

534 North Africa: Belisarius, the Byzantine general, conquers the Vandals and adds their territory to the Byzantine empire. France: The Franks conquer Burgundy.

535 Byzantine forces start the reconquest of Italy from the Ostrogoths (completed 554). India: The Gupta empire finally collapses.

540 War breaks out again between Persia and the Byzantine empire (to 562).

542 Byzantine empire: An epidemic of plague starts. It lasts until 546.

550 Wales: St David brings Christianity. He becomes the first abbot of Menevia, now known as St David's. He dies in about 601 and later becomes the patron saint of Wales.

552 Buddhism is introduced into Japan.

553 Egypt becomes part of the Byzantine empire and Justinian reforms its administration.

554 Byzantine armies conquer south-eastern Spain and add it to the empire.

561 France: Civil war breaks out among the Merovingians.

562 Japanese power ends in Korea.

563 St Columba, a monk from Ireland, founds a monastery on the island of Iona off the west coast of Scotland and begins to convert the Picts to Christianity.

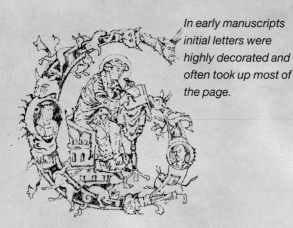

In early manuscripts initial letters were highly decorated and often took up most of the page.

565 Justinian dies and his nephew, Justin II, rules the Byzantine empire (to 578).

568 Italy: A Germanic people known as Lombards conquer the north under the leadership of their king, Alboin. In 572 he establishes the kingdom of Lombardy, with Pavia as its capital.

570 Muhammad, the Prophet of Islam, is born in Mecca.

572 The Persians take control of Arabia (to 628). A new war starts between the Byzantine empire and Persia (to 591).

WAY OF LIFE

Religious communities tried to be self-supporting. Most monks never left the monastery. They grew the crops and vegetables they needed and kept animals for milk, eggs and wool. They wove cloth for their clothes and blankets. Many monasteries had a forge where tools could be made and mended. Monks worked as potters, masons, carpenters and glaziers, constructing and repairing the monastery buildings.

Life in a monastery or convent was simple but not too harsh. Time was divided between praying, sleeping and working. Every day each monk or nun was given a loaf of bread, a measure of wine and two cooked meals. They had a roof over their heads and a bed to sleep in, as well as clothes to wear. They were also looked after if they were old or ill. This was far more than many people got in the world outside and so there was never any shortage of new members to live in monasteries or convents.

Although monks and nuns lived apart from the rest of the world in order to devote themselves to God, monasteries soon began to play an important role in everyday life. For centuries monks were almost the only people who could read or write and the only way to get an education was by taking holy orders. Not everyone who did this stayed in the monastery, however. Some became priests and went out to work in the parishes, while others became secretaries to kings and other rulers. Many monks and nuns looked after the sick and the dying, caring for them in an infirmary. They used herbs from the gardens to make medicines and prayed for people's souls when everything else failed.

NUNS

At a time when women had to obey their fathers if they were single and their husbands if they were married, becoming a nun was almost the only way they could exercise any control over their own lives. They could work and study and some had power as abbesses in charge of convents.

RULE

The Rule is the name for the guidelines along which convents and monasteries were organized. The Benedictine Rule is the best known, but in Britain it had a rival in the Rule of St Columba. He was an Irish monk who founded a monastery on Iona, off the west coast of Scotland.

▲ Many monasteries had schools and large libraries where trained monks copied out books by hand. Some of the more learned monks wrote new books as well.

Almost all monasteries provided accommodation for travellers, and especially for pilgrims who were making long journeys to holy places. Most monasteries also had a library of classical and biblical texts. These were often copied out by hand in the *scriptorium* and were the basis for much of the learning of the time. Some monks wrote histories. One of the most famous was Bede who wrote the *Ecclesiastical History of the English People* in 731.

▼ Monks spent months or even years illuminating (decorating) a manuscript with beautiful pictures. The Celtic monks of Britain and Ireland drew very individual illuminations. This page is from the Book of Kells, a copy of the Gospels begun by monks on the island of Iona in Scotland and completed in Ireland. It shows St John the Evangelist surrounded by designs which are typically Celtic in origin.

MONKS IN OTHER RELIGIONS

Christianity was not the only religion to have monks and monasteries at this time. Both the Jainist and Buddhist religions had monks who lived in monasteries. Their lives, however, were different from those of the Christian monks. Buddhist monks spent much of their time in prayer, but they did not have to be monks for all of their lives. They could leave the monastery whenever they wanted. The Jains believed that becoming a monk was the only way to escape a cycle of rebirth after death.

Sui and Tang Dynasties

The Sui dynasty was founded in 581 when Yang Chien seized the throne of north China. By sending an army across the River Yangtze and reconquering the south of the country, he was able to reunite China for the first time since the end of the Han dynasty in 220. Before he came to power, taxes were high and people were conscripted into the armies for long periods of time. Yang Chien cut both the amount of taxation and the period of conscription. He governed firmly from his capital, Chang'an, and during his rule Buddhism began to spread from India. He also encouraged agriculture by setting up irrigation schemes so that more rice and grain crops could be grown. This helped to make the country wealthy again.

The second Sui emperor was Yang Di. Under his rule, the Grand Canal was rebuilt on a large scale. He also had palaces and pleasure parks built for himself and raised money for them by ordering people to pay ten years' tax in advance. The peasants rebelled and in 618 Yang Di was killed.

Li Yuan, an official from the Sui

▲ *This pottery camel from the Tang dynasty is loaded with bales of silk, China's most important export. Chang'an at the end of the Silk Road grew to become the largest city in the world at this time.*

▼ *The Grand Canal linked the main rivers of China and made it possible to travel from the south to the north of the country without using the dangerous sea route. Because they were easier to use than roads, the waterways were the most important trading routes in China and goods of all sorts were carried along them.*

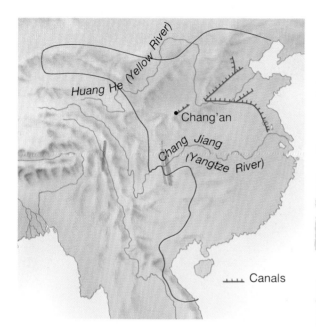

▲ *From its original boundaries (shown above) the Tang empire grew to be the largest empire in the world. An efficient canal system helped transport.*

dynasty, then founded the Tang dynasty. This lasted until 907 and was a time of Chinese excellence in the arts, science and technology. The silk trade flourished with merchants from many countries transporting cloth by land and by sea. The making of fine porcelain and gunpowder for fireworks were invented and printing was developed.

GUNPOWDER

One of the most important inventions of the Tang dynasty was gunpowder. It was made accidentally by a scientist who was trying to make a potion to give everlasting life. At first, it was made into fireworks, which were used to frighten an enemy. Later it was used in weapons.

PRINTING

By the 10th century, the Chinese were printing books using wooden blocks. These made it possible to print pictures and text, as both could be carved into the wood. It took a long time to carve each page, but it was worthwhile because many copies could then be printed.

581 China: Yang Chien, formerly chief minister of the Chou, founds the Sui dynasty and starts to reunite the country for the first time since the fall of the Han dynasty in 220.

584 England: The Anglo-Saxon kingdom of Mercia, roughly spanning the modern Midlands, is founded.

585 China: Reconstruction work starts on the Great Wall. Many thousands of people are conscripted to do the work and many of them die in the harsh conditions.

587 Spain: The Visigoths become Christians.

589 Persia: The Arabs, Khazars and Turks invade, but are defeated. China: The country is finally united under the Sui.

A pottery figure of a lady from Tang China. Tombs were filled with models of servants, animals and businessmen such as merchants and traders. The figures were meant to serve the dead person in the afterlife.

590 Gregory I, also known as Gregory the Great, becomes pope (to 604). Famous for his charitable works, after his death he is made into a saint.

593 China: The first printing press is invented. Japan: Suiko becomes empress of Japan (to 628). Buddhism takes root and becomes the official religion in 594.

594 Muhammad enters the service of Khadija, a rich widow, whom he later marries. They have six children.

596 Pope Gregory I sends Augustine to convert the Anglo-Saxons to Christianity. Legend says that this happened after Gregory saw some people who had been taken to Rome to be sold as slaves. He asked who they were and was told they were Angles. He then said 'They are not Angles, but angels'.

Buildings

Building styles varied throughout the world. In hot countries, buildings were made to shelter people from the Sun. Cold countries had buildings to protect people from wind and rain. Where trees were plentiful, houses were made entirely of wood. This was especially true in northern Europe. Even the first castles were made of wood, but they were later built in stone. In warmer climates sun-baked bricks, or adobe, were used.

Early villages developed around a spring or well. Sometimes they were surrounded by a ditch with a wooden fence on top for protection.

Many Roman towns in northern Europe were abandoned. In their place, towns developed around castles and manor houses. The houses had a solid timber frame, but their walls were made of wattle and daub (woven twigs covered with mud or plaster). In southern Europe, however, many Roman towns survived and people continued to live in their houses.

▶ A sanctuary knocker on an abbey door was so-called, because criminals could find temporary refuge there.

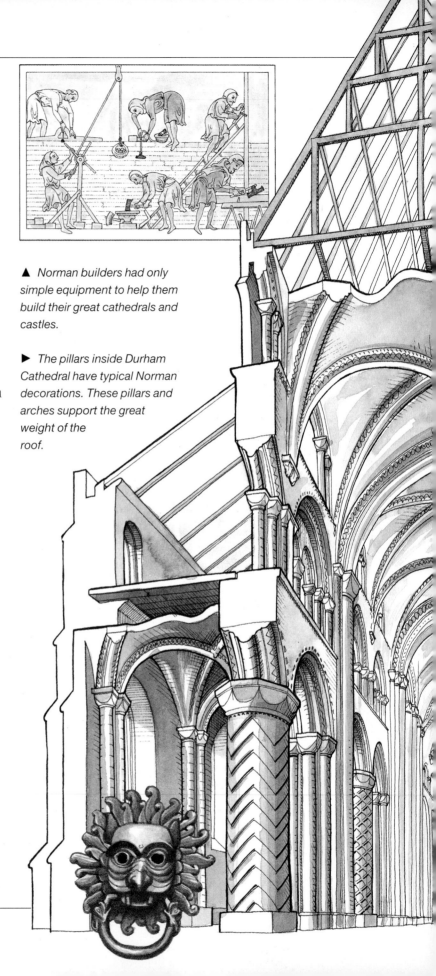

▲ Norman builders had only simple equipment to help them build their great cathedrals and castles.

▶ The pillars inside Durham Cathedral have typical Norman decorations. These pillars and arches support the great weight of the roof.

WHEN IT HAPPENED

700 In America the Anasazi people start to build pueblos, or communal villages.

7th century The first mosques are built.

1067 The Normans start to build the Tower of London to impress the defeated English.

1093 Durham Cathedral is begun.

▲ *Motte-and-bailey castles (above) were common all over western Europe. The outer wall was replaced with stone (below) to stop attackers setting fire to them.*

◄ *Most Muslims lived in hot climates and so built their mosques to be as light and airy as possible. There are over a thousand pillars in the Great Mosque at Cordoba in Spain.*

▼ *Most Anglo-Saxon settlers built their houses and barns from wood and thatched the roofs with straw or reeds. Often, houses did not last as the wood rotted. Also, fire was always a danger.*

597 St Augustine lands in England with 30 missionaries. They go to Kent where the ruler, Ethelbert I, has a Christian wife. Augustine converts Ethelbert and his people to Christianity.

7th century Ireland: Laws are passed against using women in battle. This reverses a Celtic tradition of female fighters which goes back at least 3000 years.

604 Japan: First written constitution.

605 China: Yang Di, the second Sui emperor, orders the complete rebuilding of the Grand Canal. Both men and women do the work which takes five years.

606 India: Harsha becomes emperor in the north (to 647).

610 Muhammad has a vision in which the Archangel Gabriel commands him to proclaim the one true god, Allah.

618 China: The second Sui emperor is assassinated and Li Yuan founds the Tang dynasty (until 907).

The symbol of Islam is a crescent Moon and a star. Today this symbol often appears on the flags of countries which have a majority of Muslim people.

622 Muhammad flees from persecution in Mecca to Yathrib, later called Medina. This is known as the Hegira and marks the start of the Islamic calendar.

624 Muhammad marries Aisha. China: Buddhism becomes the official religion although others are allowed.

625 Muhammad begins dictating the Koran, the holy book of Islam. The Persians attack Constantinople, but fail to take it.

626 Egypt: The Byzantine emperor Heraclius I expels the Persians.

The Foundation of Islam

The prophet Muhammad, who founded the religion called Islam, was born in Mecca in 570. At this time the Arab peoples worshipped many different gods. Muhammad, however, was influenced by the Judeo-Christian belief in just one god. When he was about 40 years old, he had a vision in which the Archangel Gabriel told him to preach about one god, who was called Allah. The word Islam means 'submission to the will of Allah'. When Muhammad started preaching in Mecca, the people felt that the new religion threatened their old gods. In 622 Muhammad and his followers had to flee to the nearby town of Medina.

In Medina, Muhammad and his followers organized the first Muslim state and built the first mosque. Muhammad taught that people could be saved through regular prayer and by avoiding the pollution of their bodies with

MUHAMMAD

Muhammad was brought up by his uncle who was the chief of a small tribe. He spent his early years looking after sheep and camels. Then he went to work for a wealthy widow called Khadija, whom he later married. He started preaching in Mecca when he was about 40 years old, but his life was threatened, so he fled to Medina in 622. His journey is known as the Hegira. This date marks the start of the Muslim calendar. There are many pictures of Muhammad, but Islamic traditions forbid artists to show his face. Because of this, he is often shown with a veil, as in this picture.

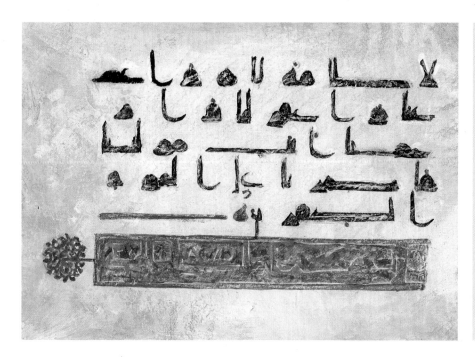

THE SPIDER

When Muhammad was fleeing from Mecca to Medina, he went into a cave to hide from his pursuers. While he was in there, a spider spun a complete web across the entrance. His pursuers saw the web and decided Muhammad could not be in the cave because otherwise it would be broken. They passed on and Muhammad was saved.

▲ *This page from the Koran was written in the 9th century. It was important to Muslims to make the words of Allah look as beautiful as possible.*

certain foods and drinks. These teachings, together with Muhammad's prophecies, were written down in the Koran, the holy book of Islam. Muhammad insisted that the words were those of Allah, speaking through him.

During his stay in Medina, Muhammad's following grew quickly. Most of the Arabian people were very poor. They were attracted to Islam because they felt its teachings offered them the chance of a fairer society.

In 630 Muhammad recaptured Mecca. He became its ruler, and banned the worship of idols. He also kept non-believers out of the city and, to this day, only Muslims are allowed into it. Under Muhammad's rule, the Islamic empire gained control of most of the Arabian peninsula. After his death in 632 the Islamic religion began to spread beyond Arabia to Europe and India.

▶ *The Dome of the Rock in Jerusalem is the third most important Muslim shrine, after Mecca and Medina. It was built over the rock from which Muhammad is said to have ascended to heaven. Completed in 691 and decorated with complex geometric patterns, it is one of the earliest Muslim buildings still in existence.*

The Islamic Empire

After Muhammad's death, Muslim armies began to spread the Islamic religion. In 633 they moved north towards the Byzantine and Sassanian empires. Although the Byzantine empire was rich and powerful, it had just fought a costly war against the Sassanians. Early in 634, the Muslim leader, Abu Bakr, called for a *jihad*, or holy war. He sent an army to Syria and defeated the Byzantine forces at Ajnadain. By the end of 635 the Arabs had conquered most of Syria and Palestine and in 636 they defeated the Byzantine army again near the River Yarmuk. Continuing the successful military expeditions the Muslims advanced east into Mesopotamia and west into Anatolia. By 643 they had gained control of Persia.

The Muslims pushed east to Afghanistan and reached India early in the 8th century. Another army headed west to capture Egypt from the Byzantines by 642. By 700 most of the north coast of Africa was under Muslim

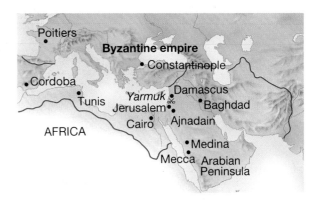

▲ *The Islamic empire spread rapidly. Its capital moved from Medina to Damascus and later to Baghdad.*

control. Berbers and Arabs from Morocco invaded Spain in 711. They did not reach the rest of Europe because they were defeated by the Franks at Poitiers in 732.

Most of the conquered peoples became Muslims and Arabic became the most important language in all parts of the Islamic empire except Persia. This helped ideas and knowledge to spread quickly from one place to another.

▼ *The Arabs were fierce and fearless warriors. At the battle of Yarmuk, an Islamic army of 25,000 men defeated 50,000 Byzantine troops.*

▲ *As well as their religion, the Arabs brought their style of architecture to the lands they conquered. Mosques were built all over the Islamic world.*

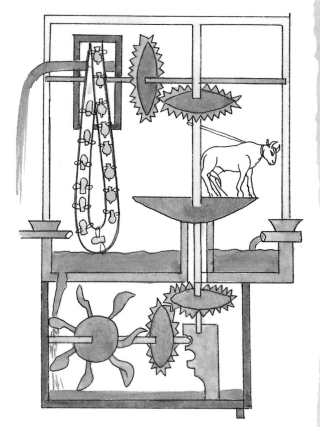

▲ *Islamic scientists built on the discoveries of Hellenistic and ancient Greece, Persia and India. Through them this knowledge spread to Europe.*

627 Near East: The Byzantine emperor Heraclius defeats the Persians at Nineveh. China: T'ai Tsung the Great becomes emperor (to 649) and there is a period of military conquest. Arts and letters also flourish at this time.

629 Dagobert I reunites the Frankish kingdom.

630 Muhammad captures Mecca, and sets out the principles of Islam.

632 Muhammad dies and is succeeded as leader of Islam by his father-in-law, Abu Bakr. He is the first caliph and leads the Muslims until his death in 634.

633 England: The Mercians under Penda defeat the Northumbrians.

634 Omar I becomes caliph of Mecca (to 644). He continues the holy war first called by Abu Bakr.

By using an astrolabe Arab sailors could plot their position at sea.

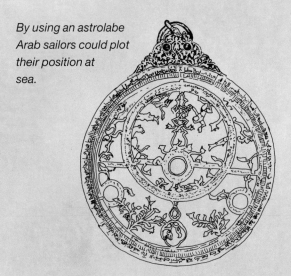

635 The Muslims begin the conquest of Syria, which takes three years, and of Persia, which takes eight years.

638 Islamic empire: The Muslims capture Jerusalem.

639 The Muslims start on their conquest of Egypt (completed in 642).

642 England: The Mercians under Penda again defeat the Northumbrians.

643 Islamic empire: The Arabs finally defeat the Persians at Nehawand.

644 Mecca: Following the assassination of Omar, Othman becomes caliph of Islam (to 656).

645 Egypt: Byzantine forces recapture Alexandria, whose people have risen against the Arabs. Japan: The Taikwa edict of reform nationalizes land in Japan and reorganizes the government. The Japanese still tend to imitate the Chinese way of life.

646 Islamic empire: The Arabs recapture Alexandria.

649 The Arabs conquer Cyprus.

c.650 The Babylonian Talmud, a record of Jewish religious law, is finalized.

655 England: Oswy, King of Northumbria, defeats and kills Penda of Mercia. Islamic empire: The Arabs have their first naval victory when they defeat the Byzantine fleet at the battle of the Masts off the Egyptian coast near Alexandria.

656 Following the assassination of Othman by supporters of Muhammad's brother-in-law Ali, Ali becomes caliph of Islam (to 661).

661 Islamic empire: Mu'awiya founds the Umayyad dynasty (to 750). Mu'awiya rules as caliph until 680.

664 England: At the Synod of Whitby, King Oswy of Northumbria abandons the Celtic Christian Church and accepts Rome's form of Christianity with the pope as its leader. The Celtic Church, which has kept Christianity alive in the west and north of Britain since the Romans left, starts to decline.

668 Korea: The kingdom of Silla reunites the country and marks the start of the Silla period which lasts until 935.

669 The Greek monk Theodore of Tarsus is sent to England as archbishop of Canterbury to reorganize the Church in England and make it like the Church in the rest of western Europe.

The Star of David, or the Shield of David, is a very ancient symbol. It first appeared as a symbol of Judaism around 960 BC.

Persecution of the Jews

After the destruction of Jerusalem in AD 70, most Jews moved into exile. In what is called the Diaspora, or dispersion, they gradually spread out all over Europe and northern Africa. Large numbers of them went to Spain, where they were called Sephardim, and Germany, where they were known as Ashkenasim. They formed small, usually separate communities in various cities and kept to their own traditions in religion and learning.

Many were skilled craftsmen, but others earned their living by trade or by money-lending. Lending with interest was forbidden to Christians, so Jews often provided an important service to European societies. Money-lending made some of the Jews unpopular, but they were usually allowed to live in peace.

By the 11th century, however, Europe had become very religious. Anyone who was not a Christian was also not part of European society. This made people turn against the Jews. They were forced to

▲ *The arrows show the approximate movement of Jewish people during the Diaspora and, later on, in the early stages of persecution in the 12th century.*

▲ *Jewish boys went to schools where they were taught by the rabbis. They kept their traditions alive by learning to read, write and speak Hebrew.*

▼ *In the persecution, many Jews were burned to death, like these in Cologne. Sometimes whole communities were wiped out in this way.*

GHETTOS

Once the persecution began, all the Jews in a city were forced to live in small areas of cities which became known as ghettos. They were usually in a poor part where nobody else wanted to live. Although the Jews were forced to stay there, the ghettos did not protect them.

YIDDISH

The Jews' own language was Hebrew. It has an alphabet of 22 letters and is written from right to left. The Ashkenasim Jews in eastern and central Europe developed a language called Yiddish. It was a mixture of German and Hebrew, but written in Hebrew letters.

live in separate areas known as ghettos.

The situation grew worse when many Christians began to blame the Jews for the death of Jesus, forgetting that Jesus himself was a Jew. As a result, Jews were persecuted, killed or expelled from their homes. Many fled east to Poland and Lithuania. In the 12th century, even the Moors in Spain turned against them and in 1290 England became the first country to expel all Jews.

ARAB TOLERATION

Because of the persecution the Jews faced from Christian rulers many of them welcomed Arab conquests which brought greater toleration. In the Near East, Spain and North Africa, especially Cairo, Jewish communities prospered. Under Islamic rule, Jews (and other recognized non-Muslim religions) enjoyed security and protection from their enemies, freedom of worship and took a large part in deciding their own affairs. But they had to pay heavier taxes than Muslims and could not bear arms.

Communications

In western Europe the Roman empire left behind a good system of roads, but over the years they were neglected and the stones used by farmers and builders, until only dirt tracks were left. This made it easier to travel on foot or on horseback than in a wheeled vehicle. In wet weather the tracks became impassable. Then, many people stayed at home or travelled by boat.

At this time, not all countries had suitable horses. Horses in China were generally small, while in America there were no horses at all until the arrival of Europeans. In Africa, camels were more suitable for journeys across the desert, but horses were used in the grasslands.

Writing flourished in the Byzantine, Islamic and Chinese empires. In northern Europe, however, it mainly survived in monasteries. Even kings such as William the Conqueror could not read or write. In court and on their travels they always dictated their letters and records of events to a scribe. Most communication was by word of mouth and so news travelled slowly.

◀ Bede was a monk at Jarrow in England. He is sometimes called the 'Father of English History'. This is because he wrote a book called the Ecclesiastical History of the English People. He was the first historian to date events from the birth of Jesus.

▼ Before printing came to Europe, all books had to be copied out by hand, which could take months or years to do. There was no paper and so animal skin, called parchment, was used. Mistakes and blots had to be scraped off with a sharp knife.

◄ Most writing was done with a quill, usually a goose feather. It was sharpened to a point and dipped in ink. It was resharpened with a little knife, later known as a pen-knife. The Chinese wrote with brushes made of horse hair.

▲ In many places it was easier to travel by water than overland. During this period the Grand Canal was rebuilt in China. It connected the main rivers and meant that people going north or south could avoid the dangerous coast. Many people made their homes on boats and lived on the canal.

▲ The earliest known printed book is the Diamond Sutra *which was printed in China in 868. The text and pictures were engraved on wooden blocks, which were then spread with ink and printed.*

WHEN IT HAPPENED

593 The Chinese start using woodblocks for printing. They have used paper for about 500 years.

618 The Sui emperor Yang Di is assassinated in China. He employed over 2,000,000 people to rebuild the Grand Canal.

731 Bede completes his *Ecclesiastical History of the English People*. It is written in Latin, but translated into English in the reign of King Alfred (871–899).

863 St Cyril is sent to Moravia to convert the Slavs to Christianity. He introduces the Cyrillic alphabet for the Slav languages.

▲ In China both horses and camels were used for transport. The native horses were very small, but in the 2nd century BC large horses were introduced from Central Asia. Known as celestial horses, they became status symbols for officials and the rich. This ornament from the Tang dynasty shows one of them.

673 The Arabs start an unsuccessful, five-year siege of Constantinople.

674 Islamic empire: The Arab conquest reaches the River Indus in what is now Pakistan.

675 The Bulgars settle south of the River Danube and found their first empire.

680 Islamic empire: Civil war breaks out among the Arabs.

685 Abdalmalik becomes caliph of Islam (to 705). In this time, he sets up a new system of administration in the Arab empire.

687 Pepin the Younger reunites the Frankish kingdom after his victory at the battle of Tertry.

A Central American funerary urn showing Cocijo, the rain god, who has a forked tongue. Funerary urns were at first carved by hand, but later on they were mass-produced using moulds.

697 North Africa: The Arabs destroy Carthage, the former Vandal capital.

700 England: The Psalms are translated into Anglo-Saxon and the Lindisfarne Gospels are started. Germany: Thuringia becomes part of the Frankish kingdom. Islamic empire: The Arabs capture Tunis and Christianity in North Africa disappears almost completely.

8th century North America: The first true towns appear. Africa: Bantu Africans cross the River Limpopo taking iron working to southern Africa.

702 The Ethiopians attack Arab ships in the Red Sea. In return, the Arabs occupy Ethiopian ports. Arabic is declared the official language of Egypt.

707 North Africa: The Arabs capture Tangier.

709 North Africa: The Arabs capture Ceuta.

710 Spain: Roderic, the last Visigothic king, comes to the throne.

North America

The first true North American towns appeared in the middle Mississippi Valley around the beginning of the 8th century. Remains of them have been found as far apart as Cahokia in Illinois, Aztalan in Wisconsin and Macon in Georgia. Now called the Temple Mound culture, each town had a central plaza with up to 20 rectangular mounds of earth arranged around it. On top of these were temples and houses for the dead. The plaza was separated from the rest of the town by a wooden fence, or palisade. Around the plaza up to 10,000 people lived in long houses with mud walls and thatched roofs. The villages were fortified and the people were farmers, growing maize (corn), sunflowers, beans and pumpkins. After about 800 they stopped using spear-throwers and darts for hunting and used bows and arrows instead.

In the south-west people known as the Anasazi started building houses above

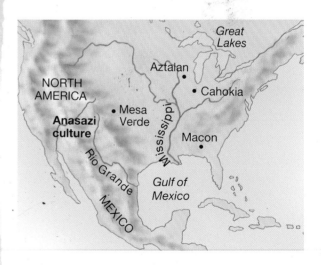

▲ *The Temple Mound culture gradually spread over much of the east of North America from the Great Lakes to the Gulf of Mexico. Many settlements were connected to each other by rivers. The pueblo builders lived in the south west.*

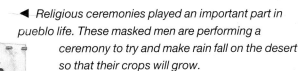

◄ *Religious ceremonies played an important part in pueblo life. These masked men are performing a ceremony to try and make rain fall on the desert so that their crops will grow.*

ground around 700. They used stone and adobe to build pueblos, which were rather like apartment blocks. By 1100 some of these were three or four storeys high and housed up to 250 people. They lived by farming. Water was valuable because there was very little rainfall. They built irrigation channels to water their crops. The villages gradually grew in size as farming improved and the Anasazi started to build *kivas* or sunken ceremonial chambers.

▼ *The Cliff Palace at Mesa Verde, Colorado, was built by the Anasazi. It housed about 250 people. The cliff sheltered it in bad weather.*

711 Spain: The Moors (Arabs and Berbers from Morocco) invade. They defeat Roderic and end the Visigothic rule.

712 Birth of Rabi-ah al-Adawiyyah, the famous female Sufi (Muslim) mystic and religious teacher (dies 801). Islamic empire: The empire expands to include Sind, which is now in Pakistan.

716 The Arabs start a second siege of Constantinople (it fails in 717). Bulgaria: The Bulgar state is recognized by the Byzantine empire.

This silver plaque is one of the few things to have survived from the once wealthy Slav kingdom of Moravia, after it was invaded by the Magyars in 899. Coins and jewellery have also been found.

718 Spain: Pelayo, a Visigoth prince, founds the kingdom of Asturias in the Spanish mountains. The Moors hold most of the rest of Spain and Portugal and advance northwards. The Christians defeat them in Spain at the battle of Covadonga.

725 Egypt: Coptic Christians rebel against Muslim rule.

726 England: King Ine of Wessex levies the first 'Peter's Pence'. This is a tax to support a religious college in Rome. Byzantine empire: Emperor Leo III begins the Iconoclast movement. This is a violent protest against sacred images and is opposed by Pope Gregory II.

730 Pope Gregory II excommunicates Leo III.

731 Bede completes his history of the Church in England.

732 France: Charles Martel, ruler of the Franks, defeats the Moors at Poitiers.

733 Byzantine empire: Emperor Leo III removes the Byzantine provinces in southern Italy from papal jurisdiction.

735 England: Death of Bede.

737 France: Charles Martel defeats the Moors again in a battle at Narbonne.

Bulgars and Russians

The people known as Slavs settled in eastern Europe and western Russia in the 8th century, after many generations of wandering across Europe. The first Slav state was in the south and was ruled by people known as Bulgars. Their state was recognized by the Byzantine empire in 716, but the two countries did not live at peace with each other. After the Bulgars had sacked Constantinople and killed the Byzantine emperor, the empire sent men to try and convert the Bulgars to Christianity. The most important were St Cyril and St Methodius. Eventually a Bulgarian king agreed to be baptized, but the quarrels did not end until the Bulgars were beaten by the Byzantines in 1014.

Other Slav communities developed in the east along many of the Russian rivers. These were ruled by Viking traders from Sweden who were known as the Rus. From this came the name Russia. The first leader of the Rus was

▲ *Vladimir, Grand Prince of Kiev, chose the Eastern Orthodox Church when he became a Christian.*

Rurik. He founded Novgorod and then Kiev, and all Russian nobility afterwards claimed to be descended from him.

In 988 the Russian prince Vladimir was converted to Christianity and married a Byzantine princess. He then forced Christianity on the rest of the Russian nobility. By the 11th century the Russian capital Kiev was a centre of splendour and influence to rival Constantinople. Its greatest ruler was Yaroslav the Wise, who set up diplomatic relations with other courts. In this period many churches were built, the first Russian laws were written, and so were the first works of Russian literature.

◀ *Most of the Slav states followed the Eastern Orthodox religion. Churches and homes were decorated with religious paintings, called icons.*

▼ *When the Bulgars killed the Byzantine emperor Nicephorus in 811, they made his skull into a goblet for Krum, who was their king or khan. The Byzantine emperors called Bulgarian kings tsars or caesars.*

CYRILLIC

In the 9th century St Cyril and his brother St Methodius invented the Cyrillic alphabet which they mostly based on the letters of the Greek alphabet. Later, Christian missionaries sent to convert the Slavic people from Constantinople and Rome spread the alphabet throughout eastern Europe and Russia.

739 Egypt: The Christian Copts rebel for a second time against their Muslim rulers.

740 India: The Gurjaru-Prathi-Nara dynasty is founded in the north (to 1036).

741 Pepin the Short succeeds his father, Charles Martel, as 'mayor of the palace'. In reality this means that he rules the Franks, but he is not yet their king.

746 The Greeks retake Cyprus from Arabs.

This gold image of Charlemagne, inset with many semi-precious stones and made in Germany, is a reliquary. It was made in about 1350 to hold parts of his skull.

750 Islamic empire: The Umayyads are overthrown and the Abbasid dynasty is founded. The capital is Baghdad.

751 Pepin the Short is crowned king of the Franks. He founds the Carolingian dynasty to replace that of the Merovingians. Italy: The Lombards, led by Aistulf, capture Ravenna from the Byzantine empire. Asia: The Arabs defeat the Chinese at Samarkand.

756 Spain: Abd al-Rahman ibn Mu'awiya establishes an independent Umayyad dynasty at Cordoba. Italy: Pepin the Short's army protects Pope Stephen III from the Lombards. The Papal States are founded.

757 England: Offa becomes king of Mercia (to 796). During his reign he builds a large earthwork, known as Offa's Dyke, from the River Dee to the River Severn, to keep the Welsh out of his kingdom.

767 Egypt: Another Coptic revolt starts. It lasts until 772.

771 Pepin's son, Charles, becomes king of the Franks (to 814). He is also known as Charlemagne or Charles the Great.

772 Charlemagne conquers Saxony in Germany and converts the people to Christianity.

Charlemagne

After the Franks invaded part of the Roman empire they settled in what is now central France. Their leader, Clovis, founded the Merovingian dynasty. When he died, the kingdom was divided between his sons, but this weakened it so much that power fell into the hands of Charles Martel, who had led the Franks against the Muslims at Poitiers. In 751 Charles' son Pepin overthrew the Merovingians and began the Carolingian dynasty. After his death in 768 his sons, Carloman and Charlemagne, inherited his kingdom. Three years later Carloman died and Charlemagne took full control.

Charlemagne soon conquered the rest of France and then extended his kingdom into what is now Germany, Italy and the Netherlands. In central Europe he forced the Saxons and the Avars to accept Christianity. He supported the pope and extended the power of the church in his own kingdom. In return, the pope recognized

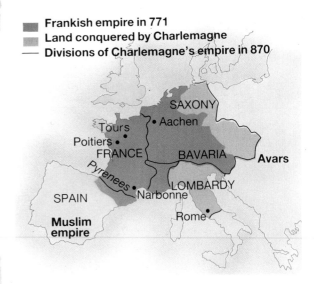

■ Frankish empire in 771
■ Land conquered by Charlemagne
— Divisions of Charlemagne's empire in 870

▲ *After Charlemagne's empire was split, the boundaries of present-day France, Italy and Germany became recognizable.*

EDUCATION

Beatissimo papae Damaso hieronimus

Scholars at Charlemagne's court in Aachen developed a new style of script for use in books. It was known as miniscule and was formed with clear, rounded letters. At this time all books were written in Latin. Charlemagne himself learned to speak and read Latin, but he did not manage to write it.

▼ *When Pope Leo III crowned Charlemagne as Holy Roman emperor in Rome on Christmas Day 800 he laid the foundations for the Holy Roman Empire which included Germany, France and part of Italy.*

Charlemagne's power in 800 by creating him Holy Roman emperor. Charlemagne also encouraged scholars by founding schools in cathedrals and monasteries. The palace school in his capital city of Aachen was the most important centre of learning in western Christendom.

After Charlemagne's death in 814, his empire was troubled by Viking raids and civil war. In 843 it was divided between his three grandsons. They and their descendants ruled Germany until 911 and France until 987.

▲ *Charlemagne was a great military leader and his kingdom became the most powerful in Europe. He also tried to improve conditions in his lands, where most of the people were poor farmers.*

Food and Farming

The use of iron tools made it possible to create a lot more farmland in this period. Iron axes could cut down bigger trees, while iron ploughs could plough heavier soils. In Britain both the Anglo-Saxons and the Vikings began to farm more and more land. When the Normans invaded, the feudal system (*see* pages 226–227) was introduced. In Europe horses and pigs were the most important animals but by 1100, sheep had become more important, because of their wool.

In China new irrigation schemes created more land for rice-growing. In North America Native Americans were settling down to grow maize (corn) in fertile river valleys.

▲ Under Norman rule, woods were cleared to provide additional farming land. People known as bordars were encouraged to set up smallholdings in clearings on the edge of woods.

▼ The development of ploughs with iron ploughshares and wheels, pulled by a team of oxen made it easier and quicker to plough through heavy soil. This meant more wheat could be sown.

▲ Grain crops were cut with a scythe (above) or a sickle (right) which had metal blades. The grain was then threshed with a wooden flail (left) to separate it from the chaff (the outer husks). When tossed up into the air, the lighter chaff blew away.

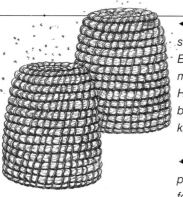

◄ Honey was the only source of sweetening in Europe at this time, so many people kept bees. Hives were often made of basketwork, and were known as skeps.

◄ Many people kept a pig, because it could forage for its own food in the woods and on common land. In winter most of the animals were killed because there was not enough food for them.

▼ The Norman system of farming, where large fields were divided up into long strips to be farmed by villeins or peasants, can still be seen in England today.

▼ In Europe, harvest was a busy time. The grain was needed for bread and beer. If there was not enough, people starved in winter.

773 Charlemagne adds the kingdom of Lombardy to his Frankish empire.

778 Spain: The Moors and the Basques defeat the Franks at the battle of Roncesvalles, in the Pyrenees.

779 England: Offa, King of Mercia, becomes king of all England.

780 Constantine VI becomes the new Byzantine emperor. He is only a child and is influenced by his mother, Irene.

782 Charlemagne summons the monk and scholar Alcuin of York to head the palace school at Aachen. This event marks the revival of learning in mainland Europe.

786 Harun al-Rashid becomes caliph of Baghdad. His rule lasts until 809.

An elaborately decorated Islamic tile from Persia (present day Iran). It was made in the 12th century and may have been used as a tombstone.

787 Papacy: The Council of Nicaea orders the restoration and use of images in churches.

788 Bavaria becomes part of Charlemagne's empire.

789 England: The first Vikings arrive. They land on the south coast and kill the messenger who is sent to meet them.

791 The Byzantine emperor Constantine VI imprisons his mother because of her cruelty, and assumes power.

793 Viking raiders attack the monastery of Lindisfarne off the coast of Northumbria. They kill some of the monks and take others away to sell as slaves. They also steal the monastery treasures. This is their first serious raid in England. The *Anglo-Saxon Chronicle* records that the people of Northumbria had been 'sorely frightened' by 'immense whirlwinds, flashes of lightning, and fiery dragons... flying in the air' just before the raid.

The Abbasid Dynasty

In 750 the Abbasid family took power from the Umayyad family and started a new dynasty of caliphs which ruled the Islamic empire until 1258. The Abbasids were descended from Muhammad's uncle, al-Abbas. Under the rule of their first caliph, al-Mansur, the Abbasids moved the capital of the empire from Damascus to the newly-founded city of Baghdad. Their most famous ruler was Harun al-Rashid who was the fifth Abbasid caliph and succeeded his brother, al-Hadi, in 786. At first he ruled with the aid of the wealthy Barmecide family, but in 803 they fell from favour and he imprisoned them all. After that date, he ruled alone.

In 791 Harun al-Rashid became involved in a war against the Byzantine empire. This war lasted until 806, when he finally defeated the Byzantines. At the same time he had to fight against rebellion in his own empire as Tunisia

---

HARUN AL-RASHID

When Harun al-Rashid became caliph in 786, he ended a decade of uncertainty and rivalry in the Islamic empire. The military had backed his older brother, al-Hadi, but the officials wanted Harun to become caliph. When al-Hadi died suddenly, it was rumoured that Harun had plotted to murder him, but this was never proved. Harun soon won the support of the military and brought political unity to his empire. He is even thought to have sent ambassadors to the court of Charlemagne. After Harun's death, however, rival caliphates appeared in Spain and North Africa, but the world of Islam was still bound together by its rich culture.

ISLAMIC ART

At a time when Christian countries were often divided by disagreements between popes and emperors, Islam and its culture flourished. Muslim artists concentrated on intricate designs and beautiful handwriting. They decorated books, tiles and pottery, such as this Persian bowl.

began a struggle for independence, but he managed to defeat this, too.

In spite of these wars, Harun al-Rashid found time to encourage learning and the arts. His court was also a centre for the Islamic culture which unified the empire. It was his court in Baghdad that was the setting for many of the stories told in *The Thousand and One Nights* which are still enjoyed today. Legend says that the stories were written by a woman called Sheherezade. She married a king who had been so unhappy with all his other wives that he had killed each one on the first morning after their wedding. Sheherezade prevented this by telling the king a different story every night.

► *Arab traders carried cargo and passengers across the Indian Ocean in ships called* dhows. *They also helped to spread Islamic culture and ideas.*

▲ *The stories for* The Thousand and One Nights *came from many different countries, including India, Syria and Egypt. The stories feature Ali Baba, Sinbad the Sailor and Aladdin.*

796 England: The death of Offa ends Mercian supremacy.

797 The Byzantine empress Irene has her son Constantine blinded and then rules by herself (deposed 802).

800 onwards Europe: Feudalism (*see* pages 224–225) is established by the Franks mainly for military purposes. Horses start to be bred as big as possible for war. The lateen (or triangular) sail comes into use in the Mediterranean. It makes it possible for boats to beat into the wind. Africa: The trans-Sahara trade grows between west and north Africa. Cities such as Gao develop. Ghana is known as the 'Land of Gold' because of its growing wealth. India: The north is divided into many little states.

A beautiful gold Viking ring. Viking chiefs often gave rings or swords as a reward.

800 Pope Leo III crowns Charlemagne Holy Roman emperor of the west, recognizing his protection and expansion of Christian Europe. Germany: The Vikings invade.

802 England: Egbert becomes king of Wessex (to 839).

803 Islamic empire: Harun al-Rashid suddenly ends the power of the Barmecide family in Baghdad.

813 Mamun the Great becomes caliph of Baghdad (to 834). His 20-year reign is a great period for art and also a time of liberal religious attitudes.

814 Louis the Pious, son of Charlemagne, inherits the Frankish empire (rules to 840). During his reign the political importance of his empire declines.

The Kingdom of Ghana

The ancient kingdom of Ghana was much further north than the present country of that name. It was probably founded in the 4th century and was first ruled by the Maga dynasty. The Maga were a Berber family, but most of the people of Ghana were from the Soninke tribes. In 770 the Soninke ousted the Maga dynasty and began to build up an empire. This grew under the rule of Kaya Maghan Sisse who was king around 790. Its capital was Koumbi Saleh which was populated by Africans and by Berbers, who by this time had become Muslims.

The empire grew rich on trade and commerce and in the 9th century Arab traders described it as 'the land of gold'. The gold came from Asante and Senegal to the south and west. To the north was the Sahara Desert and many of the routes across it from the Near East and the Mediterranean ended in Ghana.

ETHIOPIA

Ethiopia became a Christian country in 350, but after Egypt became Muslim in 642, it was cut off from the main centres of Christianity for 800 years. In the Middle Ages a legend grew up about a king called Prester John who was said to rule over a Christian empire in the heart of Africa. Many Europeans thought that Ethiopia was this country and later on medieval explorers and emissaries of the pope were sent to try to find him.

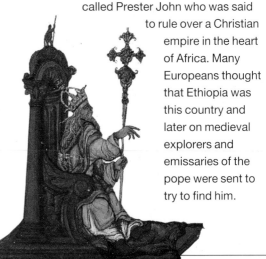

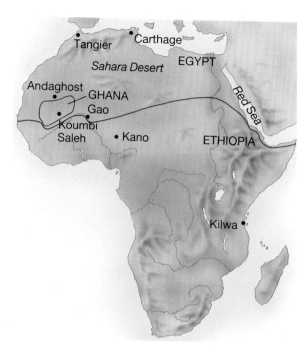

Ghana reached the peak of its powers in the 10th century when it controlled both the gold and the salt trade. Other goods which passed through Ghana included woollen cloth and luxury items from Europe, and leather goods and slaves from countries to the south. In 990 Ghana took over the Berber kingdom of Andaghost and at its greatest extent was 800 kilometres across. In 1070, however, Ghana fell to the Berber family of Almoravids and much later, in 1240, it became part of the Mali empire.

▲ Some important places in Africa during this period. By 1100 most of North Africa was Muslim, as indicated by the blue line on the map.

▼ Arab traders transported goods across the Sahara Desert on camels. They went in large groups called caravans and could travel 300 kilometres in a week.

SALT

Salt was an essential commodity, found in vast quantities in the desert. A huge trade network was set up to bring it to Ghana by camel. From here it was then taken to countries further south on horseback.

SLAVES

People captured in southern Africa were brought to Ghana to be sold as slaves. Arab traders took them across the Sahara to be sold again as servants to rich people in the Mediterranean and Near East.

Scotland

The early inhabitants of Scotland formed a number of tribes, each with its own leader. Very little is known about them until the 7th century when some of the tribes united to make two kingdoms north of a line joining the Clyde to the Forth. These kingdoms were Pictavia, which was the land of the people known as Picts, and Dalriada, which was a Christian kingdom made up of people called Scots who had come originally from Ireland. In the south, the Britons colonized the west, which they called Strathclyde, and the Angles settled in the east, which they called Bernicia. Vikings settled in the far north and west.

In 843 Kenneth MacAlpin, King of the Scots, also claimed the throne of Pictavia because his grandmother had been a Pictish princess. This united all the land north of the Clyde and Forth and it became known as Scotland. By 1018 Kenneth's successors, Kenneth II and Malcolm II, had united most of present-

▲ While the king of Scotland ruled the mainland, many of the islands were occupied by Viking people. In time these people too became part of Scotland.

▼ Many Vikings moved to the Orkney and Shetland islands in the 9th century. They lived by farming and by trading with their Viking neighbours. Their ruler was the king of Norway and the islands became the centre of the Norwegian empire based on the North Sea.

day Scotland. Malcolm's son, Duncan, was killed by a chief called Macbeth in a battle at Bothnagowan in 1040. Macbeth then ruled Scotland until he was killed by Duncan's son, Malcolm III, in 1057. Malcolm III was called Cranmore meaning 'big head'. He married a Saxon, Margaret, who was later canonized as a saint. In 1072 he became a vassal of the English king, William the Conqueror. This did not stop Malcolm raiding England, where he was killed in 1093.

BODY PAINT

The Romans gave the name Picts to all the people who lived north of a line from the Clyde to the Forth. The name means 'painted people' and the Romans used it because the Picts tattooed their bodies with patterns in different coloured vegetable dyes.

MACBETH

Macbeth became king in 1040 after killing Duncan in revenge for the murder of his brother-in-law. Macbeth ruled for 17 years and was a strong and good king.

▶ *The Scots moved to western Scotland from Ireland and forced the Picts to move further east. They were fierce warriors who dressed like the man in this picture and they were the first people in Scotland to accept Christianity. In the 8th century the Picts claimed all Scotland from their court at Scone, but in the 9th century the king of the Scots was powerful enough to claim the Pictish throne and united northern Scotland.*

817 Louis the Pious divides the Frankish empire between his sons Lothair, Pepin and Louis the German. In 829 a share is also given to his fourth son, Charles the Bald.

828 England: Egbert of Wessex is recognized as overlord of the other English kings.

835 The start of 15 years of Viking attacks on England.

839 England: Ethelwulf, son of Egbert, becomes king of Wessex (to 858).

840 Lothair I is emperor of the Franks (to 855), but his brothers are allied against him. Central Europe: Under Mojmir, a confederation of Slav tribes is formed in Bohemia, Moravia, Slovakia, Hungary and Transylvania.

The monastery on the island of Iona, off west Scotland.

841 Ireland: The Vikings start to build bases, called *long-phorts*, where they stay over winter. The earliest is Dublin, which soon attracts merchants and craftsmen. The others are Limerick, Cork, Wexford and Waterford. China: Wu Tsung persecutes all religions except Buddhism (to 846).

843 The Treaty of Verdun leads to the division of the Frankish, or Holy Roman, Empire. Louis the German rules east of the River Rhine, Charles the Bald rules France, and Lothair rules Italy, Provence, Burgundy and Lorraine. Scotland: Kenneth MacAlpin, King of the Scots, defeats the Picts and unites the country.

850 England: The Vikings stay over winter for the first time. Vikings from Sweden go to Russia. Africa: The Bantu build Great Zimbabwe.

People

Most people dressed for comfort, not fashion. In northern Europe the women wove woollen and linen cloth and made it into simple garments for their families. Men began to wear trousers made from either cloth or leather, with a tunic or doublet over the top. Women wore long dresses with belts and shawls. Both men and women wore cloaks in cold weather. People who lived in hot climates wore long, flowing clothes and cotton began to be used. In southern Europe, Roman fashions still influenced the way people dressed.

Clothing in the Byzantine empire was very decorative. Crowns decorated with pearls and precious stones were later a model for the crowns of northern rulers. In China rich people wore thin silk robes with long sleeves in hot weather and thick silk ones when it was cold.

▲ During the 11th century many people wore clothes made from sheep's wool. First, the wool was combed and spun. Then it was dyed with vegetable dyes and woven. This meant that checks, stripes and other patterns such as tartans could be woven into the fabric.

▼ Many people had leather shoes or boots. Only the poorest had to go barefoot.

▲ Ironing boards were used during this period. The stone was known as a smoothing stone.

◄ Viking jewellery was often practical. Two large brooches held together a woman's tunic while a chain held keys, scissors and a comb.

WHEN IT HAPPENED

529 St Benedict founds the order of Benedictine monks. Monasteries become an important part of medieval life.

c. 750 The feudal system appears in Europe. It changes the lives of many people and leads to stricter government of countries.

9th century Vikings who visit Constantinople start to wear Arab-style clothing.

11th century In Song dynasty China, people believe small feet are a sign of great beauty. Girls' feet are bound so they will not grow.

▲ *Chinese men and women were entertained separately. They sat on the floor or on little stools. These Tang court ladies are listening to a music concert.*

▶ *In cold climates, life centred around the hearth, placed in the middle of the room. It gave out heat and light and was also used for cooking meals. The family would sit around the fire when carrying out their daily tasks.*

851	The crossbow is used in France.
855	Louis II, son of Lothair, becomes emperor of the Franks until 875. Lothair's lands are again divided.
858	England: Ethelbald, eldest son of Ethelwulf is king of Wessex (to 860). Japan: Fujiwara Yoshifusa is regent.
860	England: Ethelbert, second son of Ethelwulf is king of Wessex (to 865). Iceland: Norwegian Vikings arrive.

Japanese horses wore many ornaments, especially bells, on their harnesses. This horse bell would probably have been worn on the horse's hindquarters.

862	Russia: Swedish Vikings, led by Rurik, seize power in the north and found a trading post at Novgorod. From there they attack Constantinople.
865	England: Ethelred I, third son of Ethelwulf, rules Wessex (to 871).
867	England: Viking invaders conquer Northumbria, East Anglia and Mercia. Photius, head of the Eastern Orthodox Church, quarrels with the pope. In 879 they excommunicate each other.
869	Malta is part of the Islamic empire.
871	England: The Danes attack Wessex. Ethelred defeats them at Ashdown. Later Ethelred dies and his brother Alfred becomes king of Wessex (to 899).
874	The Vikings settle in Iceland.
875	Charles the Bald becomes emperor of the Franks (to 877). Anarchy (disorder) follows his death.
878	England: Alfred defeats the Danes at Edington. By the Treaty of Wedmore, England is divided into Wessex in the south and the Danelaw in the north. The Vikings can live in the Danelaw on condition that they become Christians.

Fujiwara Japan

From the beginning of the 4th century, Japan was ruled by an emperor. If an emperor died while his oldest son was still very young, a regent was chosen to help the child rule. The regent was usually from the emperor's family. In the 9th century the Fujiwara family became very important at the Japanese court when Fujiwara Yoshifusa's daughter married the emperor. When the emperor died in 858, their son became emperor in his place. Fujiwara Yoshifusa then became the first regent from outside the imperial family. This was the start of what is called the Fujiwara period in Japan.

More Fujiwara daughters were married to emperors and the power of the Fujiwara family grew. Soon it became customary for every emperor to have a Fujiwara regent. While the regent controlled the running of the country, the emperor spent his time on religious matters. For three centuries the Fujiwara

▼ *Court life was very formal, with rules for everything. This man is reading a letter. Even the colour of the paper and the way it was folded were very important.*

family dominated the imperial court.

During the Fujiwara period art and literature flourished in Japan. Many people wrote poetry and some of the ladies at the court wrote books which are still read in Japan today. Families who were in favour with the Fujiwaras prospered until late in the 11th century. Then other families began to grow more powerful. These families fought among themselves and the Fujiwaras could not control them any longer. In the 12th century there were many rebellions until finally war broke out and the Fujiwara period ended.

▼ *This clay figure is of a god who protected holy buildings from demons. Most Japanese people practised the Shinto religion. This was influenced by Buddhism which was used for funerals and other ceremonies. The clothing worn by this figure is typical of a Japanese warrior from the 8th century.*

THE TALE OF GENJI

Japanese courtiers spent a lot of time entertaining each other. A novel called *The Tale of Genji* tells us a great deal about the sort of life they led. It was written by Lady Murasaki who was a lady-in-waiting to an 11th century empress. She wrote the story to be read out in instalments. At this time, many women were novelists, diarists or poets.

GARDENS

Buddhist gardens in Japan were very distinctive. They were usually set out to the south of the house and were rectangular or oval. Each had a narrow pond or lake with an island in the middle. Usually a man-made hill and waterfall stood on the northern shore of the lake.

EARTHQUAKES

During the Fujiwara period the capital city, Kyoto, suffered many fires and earthquakes. Many people thought these were caused by the spirits of officials who had been banished by the Fujiwaras. To calm the spirits, shrines were built and offerings made to them.

Magyars and Bohemians

The Magyars were a race of people who came from the steppes (open plains) of Russia, between the River Volga and the Ural Mountains. Under their leader, Prince Arpad, they entered what we now call Hungary in the late 9th century. This was a fertile area where wheat and grape vines had been grown since Roman times. This area also had rich veins of gold and silver.

Although the Magyars only numbered around 25,000 they soon defeated the local inhabitants. They raided their neighbours for slaves and treasures and also harassed the kingdom of Germany. After the German king, Otto I, defeated them at the battle of Lechfeld in 955, however, they decided to make peace. In the year 1000, Pope Sylvester crowned Stephen as the first king of Hungary. He unified the country and introduced

▲ The Slav states of Bohemia, Moravia and Poland looked to western Europe for their culture while the rest were strongly influenced by Byzantine culture.

▼ The Magyars' arrival in Hungary is shown in a manuscript called the Kepes Kronika. It shows the army accompanied by groups of women and children and cattle. Set in a flower-strewn landscape, the picture gives a peaceful impression, at odds with the Magyars' reputation as fierce warriors and raiders.

▲ *According to Hungarian tradition, this crown was given to King Stephen by Pope Sylvester at his coronation on Christmas Day 1000, as a reward for converting his people to Christianity.*

WENCESLAS

Wenceslas became prince of Bohemia in 921. He tried to make his people Christian. His brother opposed him and killed him in 929. Later Wenceslas was made a saint.

HORSEMANSHIP

The Magyars were expert horsemen. They came from the flat Russian steppe where the nature of the countryside made riding easy. Their skills on horseback helped them to go raiding in central France and Italy. They also fought on horseback and could usually outride their enemies.

880 Italy: The Byzantine emperor Basil drives the Arabs out of the mainland.

881 Charlemagne's empire (except Burgundy) is reunited when the emperor of Germany, Charles III, becomes king of the Franks.

886 England: Alfred recaptures London from the Danes.

889 Hungary: The Magyars led by Arpad invade the Hungarian plain.

890 Nailed horseshoes are used for the first time. They protect horses' feet and so longer journeys can be made. The shoes are cheap enough for peasants to afford them for their farm horses.

891 A history of England known as the *Anglo-Saxon Chronicle* starts under Alfred's instructions.

893 France: Charles the Simple becomes king. He reigns until 929.

899 England: Alfred the Great dies and Edward the Elder is king of Wessex (to 924). Moravia: Magyars from the east invade.

The Magyars rode strong horses, which could cover many miles. This helped the Magyars to carry out their devastating raids.

900 Central America: The Mayas emigrate into Yucatán. North America: The Vikings arrive in Greenland. Spain: Alfonso III of Castile begins to reconquer the country from the Moors. Europe: Castles become seats of the nobility. In eastern Europe, the Bulgars accept the Eastern Orthodox Church. Africa: The Hausa kingdom of Daura is founded in northern Nigeria. Zimbabwe in southern Africa becomes a major power. Islamic empire: The tales of *The Thousand and One Nights* are started.

Christianity to it. His reign was a time of peace and prosperity and, after his death, he was made into a saint.

North of Hungary were the Slav states of Moravia and Bohemia. In the 9th century Bohemia was part of the Moravian empire, but in 1029 Bohemia became stronger and made Moravia part of its kingdom. Christianity, introduced in the 9th century, was not completely accepted until the country came under the influence of the Holy Roman Empire.

Anglo-Saxon Britain

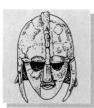

After the Romans left Britain in the 5th century, Germanic peoples began invading the country. The Jutes settled mainly in Hampshire, Kent and the Isle of Wight while the Angles and Saxons had by 600 settled most of the rest of England. The invasions pushed many of the Romano-British people into Wales and Ireland.

England was divided into seven kingdoms: Essex, Wessex and Sussex, which were ruled by the Saxons; East Anglia, Mercia and Northumbria, which were ruled by Angles; and Kent which was ruled by the Jutes.

These kingdoms often fought battles to decide which one of them had authority over all the others and claim the title *Bretwalda* (Lord of Britain) for their king. In the 7th century the Northumbrian kings Edwin, Oswald and Oswy claimed supremacy, while in the 8th century the Mercian kings Ethelbald and Offa claimed to be in control.

In 789, however, the first Vikings appeared in England and by the 850s they had started to settle. When Alfred became king of Wessex in 871, the Vikings were threatening to overrun his kingdom and he fought nine battles against them in one year. He finally

▲ *The Angles, Jutes and Saxons were skilled metal-workers who used iron for tools and weapons. They also used bronze, gold and silver to decorate items such as this helmet from around 625.*

▼ *Most of the invaders were farmers looking for new land. Their society was divided into three classes – noblemen, churls (yeomen or freemen) and slaves. In this picture, farm workers are harvesting corn.*

▲ *The seven kingdoms of England. From 878 Northumbria, East Anglia and much of Mercia came under Viking control and formed the Danelaw.*

defeated them in 878, and made them sign the Treaty of Wedmore. This allowed the Vikings to live in the north and east of the country, which became known as the Danelaw. Alfred ruled the rest. The Danelaw was gradually won back from the Vikings, and the last Viking king of York died in 954. From that date, England was one kingdom.

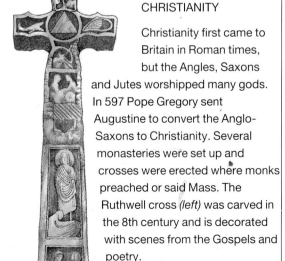

CHRISTIANITY

Christianity first came to Britain in Roman times, but the Angles, Saxons and Jutes worshipped many gods. In 597 Pope Gregory sent Augustine to convert the Anglo-Saxons to Christianity. Several monasteries were set up and crosses were erected where monks preached or said Mass. The Ruthwell cross *(left)* was carved in the 8th century and is decorated with scenes from the Gospels and poetry.

901 England: Edward the Elder takes the title 'King of the Angles and Saxons'.

906 Germany: The Magyars, from the area around the River Volga, begin invading.

907 Russia: Commercial treaties are made between Kiev and Constantinople. Silks, spices and silver from the east are traded for slaves and furs from the north. China. The fall of the Tang dynasty leads to civil wars which last until 960. At the same time, the Mongols begin their capture of Inner Mongolia and northern China (completed 1126).

909 Islamic empire: The Fatimids start to conquer north Africa by seizing power in Tunisia. They claim descent from Muhammad's daughter, Fatima, and found the Fatimid dynasty (to 1171).

This lion, symbol of St Mark, is taken from the manuscript used by the Anglo-Saxon monk St Willibrod on his travels as a missionary.

910 France: Cluny Abbey is founded. It becomes the centre of the Cluniac order which later builds monasteries in other parts of western Europe.

911 France: The King of France grants Normandy to the Viking Rollo and his followers, on condition that they help to keep the other Vikings out of the country.

912 Rollo is baptized with the name Robert.

913 England: Edward the Elder recaptures Essex from the Danes.

916 Africa: The Arab scholar, al-Masudi, travels from the Gulf down the African coast as far as Mozambique.

Religion

At the beginning of this period, only some parts of Europe were Christian. The Vikings, together with the Angles, Saxons and Jutes, had many different gods. The main Viking ones were Odin, Thor and Frey. Some early Vikings also worshipped Tyr. The Angles, Saxons and Jutes had the same gods, but called Odin, Woden, and Tyr was called Tiw. From the names of these four gods, we get Tuesday, Wednesday, Thursday and Friday. By 1100, however, the whole of Europe had accepted Christianity, though the old gods were often remembered in place names. Beyond Europe, Buddhism had begun to spread north and east from India. It became the official religion of Japan in 594 and China in 624.

In Arabia, Muhammad, the founder of Islam, was born in Mecca in 570. He started preaching about Allah, the one true god, after a dream in which the Archangel Gabriel spoke to him. After Muhammad's death in 632, his followers carried his teachings to other countries and built up an Islamic empire which stretched from Spain to northern India.

▲ A Viking cremation was described by the Arab ambassador Ibn Fadlan. On the ship with the body was food and belongings for the next life and a slave girl who was sacrificed. The pyre was lit by his nearest relative, who was naked.

▲ Muslims believe that the Archangel Gabriel was Allah's messenger. In this painting from Baghdad, Gabriel is dressed as a Muslim.

▶ Before they became Christians, the Angles buried their kings in ships with their possessions, like this gold clasp from the famous burial at Sutton Hoo. They believed that the treasures would go with the king to the afterlife.

▶ During the Sui dynasty, Buddhism became the official religion of China. Over 100,000 statues of Buddha were made, some carved out of solid rock. Many of them showed Buddha with a laughing face. Almost 4000 temples were built in this period. There were also many temples in caves along the Silk Road.

WHEN IT HAPPENED

532	Justinian starts to build the church of St Sophia in Constantinople.
622	Muhammad's flight to Medina marks the start of the Islamic calendar.
632	Muhammad dies.
664	King of Northumbria accepts the Roman Catholic Church, abandoning Celtic one.
1000	The Vikings in Iceland become Christian.
1096	The First Crusade to the Holy Land starts.

▶ Odin was the chief of the Viking gods. Legend says that he lost his eye to gain knowledge in payment for a drink at the Well of Knowledge. Tales also say he owned two ravens, Thought and Memory. He sent them out daily to report on happenings in the world. He rode an eight-legged horse called Sleipnir.

The Holy Roman Empire

 Although the idea of a Holy Roman Empire was founded by Charlemagne in 800, the land he ruled was usually called the Carolingian empire. Its area covered present-day France, Austria, Germany and Switzerland, but after his death the empire gradually broke up and France became separated.

Otto I, who became king of Germany in 936, wanted to revive the old Roman empire. In 962 he had the pope crown him Emperor Augustus, founding a line of emperors which lasted until 1806. Otto was a powerful ruler who brought stability by subduing his vassals (the

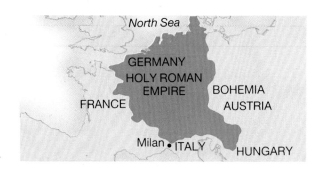

▲ By 1100 the Holy Roman Empire stretched from the North Sea and the Baltic, nearly to the Mediterranean. At this time it was ruled from Germany.

▼ The Holy Roman emperor had the right to be crowned by the pope in Rome. However, many emperors and popes disagreed with each other over questions of authority. This led to problems, especially if one side wanted to interfere in the other's affairs.

▲ *Otto I, also known as Otto the Great, came to the throne of Germany in 936. He gave a lot of land to the bishops to try to limit the power of the nobles.*

nobility who owed him allegiance) and defeating the Magyars. He conquered Bohemia, Austria and north Italy. His empire became the Holy Roman Empire.

The empire was made up of many separate duchies, counties and bishoprics (districts ruled by a bishop). Although they all owed allegiance to the emperor, they were independent of each other. After Otto died there were clashes as one or another struggled for power. The emperor was chosen by members of the nobility called electors, but they usually 'chose' the king of Germany.

The popes who helped to create the Holy Roman Empire thought that its emperors would help them to rule over Christendom. Instead, the powerful Holy Roman emperors were often in dispute with the popes and were sometimes even at war with them.

918 England: Aethelflaed, daughter of King Alfred dies. During his reign this 'Lady of the Mercians' helped to unite England by rebuilding the fortifications of Chester and building new fortified towns, including Warwick and Stafford. She fought in Wales and led her own troops to capture Derby from the Vikings. She also received the peaceful submission of Leicester and York.

A Peruvian pottery figure of a god made between 600 and 1000. Its body is decorated with maize (corn). Most Peruvians were farmers and worshipped many different land gods.

919 Germany: Henry I, or Henry the Fowler, becomes king (till 936).

920 Africa: The golden age of the kingdom of Ghana begins. It lasts until 1050.

922 North Africa: The Fatimids seize power in Morocco.

924 England: Athelstan, son of Edward the Elder, becomes king of Wessex. He annexes Northumbria, and forces the kings of Wales, Strathclyde and Scotland to submit to him.

929 Bohemia: Wenceslas, attempting to convert his people to Christianity by asking German missionaries to come to Bohemia, is murdered by his younger brother, Boleslav, a pagan.

930 Spain: Cordoba becomes the seat of Arab learning.

935 Korea: Rebel leader Wanggon overpowers the Silla and founds the state of Koryo from which the name Korea is derived. The Koryo period lasts until 1392.

936 Germany: Otto I, King of Germany, revives the Holy Roman Empire. In 962 he has himself crowned Emperor Augustus. He reigns until 973.

The Americas

Apart from the Vikings' brief visits around 1003, the peoples of the Americas remained isolated from the rest of the world. By 900 the city-state of Teotihuacán in the highlands had been destroyed and Mexico was overrun by barbarian tribes from the north. In 968 one of these tribes, the Toltecs, established their capital at Tula. It became the centre of a military state and a trading network which reached as far as Panama and Colombia. They invaded the Mayas (*see* pages 150–151) and built new administrative centres, such as Chichén Itzá, in Yucatán. The Toltecs' kings were also their religious leaders and one of them was called Topiltzin Quetzalcoatl. Legend says that he was driven out of Tula by a rival religious group and sailed east, vowing to return one day. The Toltec empire ended in the 12th century and the city of Tula was destroyed.

The great civilizations in South America at this time were based in the Andes Mountains and along the coast of Peru. One was based on Tiahuanaco, a large city and ceremonial site near Lake Titicaca in what is now Bolivia. Up to

▲ These earrings are from Huari. They are 4.6 centimetres in diameter and are made from stone. The pattern is made from pieces of bone and shell, carefully inlaid into the stone. The people of Huari also made jewellery and fine small objects out of gold.

▶ The Toltec empire was arranged along military lines. The temples in their capital of Tula were guarded by stone statues of warriors like this one. The Toltecs believed in a god called Quetzalcóatl, the 'plumed serpent', who was the legendary founder of Tula.

▼ This stepped stone pyramid was built at Chichén Itzá. It combines both Mayan and Toltec styles.

100,000 people lived there when the city was at its greatest between 600 and 1000. The people of Tiahuanaco made distinctive pottery and jewellery.

The other great South American civilization was based on the city of Huari. Unlike Tiahuanaco, Huari was the centre of a powerful military empire, covering more than half of modern Peru. Both cities had many stone temples decorated with intricate carvings and may have followed the same religion. They did not know how to smelt iron so they made axes and other tools from flint. The two cities prospered for over two centuries until about 1000 when they were suddenly abandoned.

▲ The civilizations of Central and South America had no contact with other parts of the world. Contact between them was limited by the large areas of thick jungle which covered the narrow width of Central America. They built great stone pyramids, studied mathematics and astronomy and used a calendar.

A 12th century pottery bowl from New Mexico. The hole in the centre was made on purpose to 'kill' the dish so that it could then be buried with the dead.

937 Britain: At the battle of Brunanburh, Athelstan defeats an alliance of Scots, Celts, Danes and Vikings, and takes the title of 'King of all Britain'.

939 England: Athelstan dies and his brother, Edmund, becomes king of England. In Japan the first of a series of civil wars starts.

942 Scotland: Malcolm I is king (to 953).

943 England: Dunstan becomes abbot of Glastonbury. He rebuilds its monastery and starts a revival of monasticism in England.

945 Britain: The Scots annex Cumberland and Westmorland from the English.

946 England: Edmund is assassinated and his younger brother Edred becomes king (to 955). He appoints Dunstan as his chief minister.

950 Otto I, King of Germany, conquers Bohemia. Europe: The invention of the padded horse-collar means horses can pull heavier loads and wagons. Central America: Yucatán is invaded by the Toltecs, who take control of Chichén Itzá.

951 Otto I campaigns in Italy.

954 England: Eric Bloodaxe, the last Viking king to rule in York, is killed at the battle of Stainmore.

955 England: Edwy, son of Edmund, becomes king until 959. Germany: Otto I defeats the Magyars at Lechfeld and stops their westward expansion.

956 Edwy sends Dunstan into exile.

957 Mercia and Northumbria rebel against Edwy.

959 Edgar the Peaceful, younger brother of Edwy, becomes king of England (to 975). He recalls Dunstan from exile and makes him archbishop of Canterbury.

Popes and Emperors

At this time, the most important ruler in western Europe was the pope. As head of the Roman Catholic Church, he was in charge of a wealthy organization. The Church owned vast areas of land and had estates in many different countries. In addition to this, the Roman Catholic Church had become the only church in Western Europe. All the people had to obey the pope and so he could influence the way the leaders of countries behaved. Eventually this power led to conflict between the popes and the rulers of the Holy Roman Empire. Strong popes thought they had the right to choose the emperor and strong emperors thought they had the right to choose the pope.

Emperor

Pope

Nobility

High clergy

▼ In disputes between popes and emperors the emperor relied on the support of the nobility. However they sometimes rebelled against him.

▲ In disputes the pope was supported by most of the bishops and the abbots and, through them, monks and priests.

Soldiers

Farmers

▲ The noblemen usually supported the emperor against the pope, but sometimes they rebelled against him. The knights and soldiers supported the baron, or nobleman, who gave them their land.

Monks

▶ The disputes had little effect on the daily lives of peasants, the majority of the population. They were more worried about producing enough food to keep themselves alive and keeping a roof over their heads.

Labourers

▲ *When the Holy Roman emperor Henry IV went to see the pope at Canossa, Gregory kept him waiting outside for three days in a snow storm before forgiving him and removing the ban of excommunication.*

The Holy Roman emperors tried to control the Church's affairs in their lands. They wanted the right to choose bishops but the Church disagreed. In the 1070s this led to a big dispute between Emperor Henry IV and Pope Gregory VII over who should become the next archbishop of Milan. This was an important post in the Church. It was also important to the Holy Roman Empire as Milan controlled the mountain passes between Germany and Italy. In 1075 Gregory said Henry had no right to choose any of the bishops. In revenge, Henry said that Gregory was no longer pope. Since not many people supported Henry in this, Gregory excommunicated him. This meant Henry was no longer a member of the Church and would go to Hell after he died. It also meant his subjects did not have to obey him. In 1077 Henry went to the pope and asked to be forgiven. The quarrel over choosing bishops was finally settled in 1122. There were many more disputes over land and power, and neither side ever really won.

960 Poland: Mieszko I becomes the first ruler (to 992). China: The Song dynasty is founded (to 1279).

961 The German king Otto I makes another expedition to Italy to protect the pope.

962 Pope John XII crowns Otto emperor in Rome, reviving the Holy Roman Empire.

966 Holy Roman Empire: Otto I makes a third expedition to Italy. His son, Otto II, is crowned as future emperor.

971 Scotland: Kenneth II becomes king to 995.

973 Otto II is Holy Roman emperor to 983.

975 England: Edward the Martyr, son of Edgar, becomes king until 978.

976 China: T'ai Tsung starts to reunite the country. It takes until 979 to complete.

978 England: Edward the Martyr is murdered at Corfe Castle. He is succeeded as king by his younger brother, Ethelred II, also known as the Redeless. China: The writing of an encyclopedia in 1000 volumes begins.

980 England: The Danes raid again, attacking Chester and Southampton. East Africa: The Arabs begin settling along the coast.

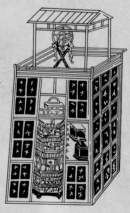

An astronomical clock built during the Song dynasty in China. It was powered by a controlled flow of water over a wheel. The hours were marked by the striking of an internal gong.

983 Venice and Genoa start trading with Asia.

985 North America: The Viking, Eric the Red, sets out from Iceland with 25 ships of people who want to settle in the land he has called Greenland to make it attractive to them. Denmark: Sweyn Forkbeard is king (to 1014).

Science and Technology

Many advances in science and technology were made by the Chinese and the Arabs. The Chinese knew how to make medicines from herbs, and understood how vaccination worked. They also made a magnetic compass and invented gunpowder for fireworks and as a signalling device. The Chinese progressed from using wooden blocks for printing to using movable type.

The Arabs were skilled at astronomy and mathematics, and used the decimal system of numbers which had been invented in India. They drew the most accurate maps available at that time. They knew how lenses worked and, like the Chinese, they made herbal medicines to treat people. Cairo in Egypt, and Baghdad in Mesopotamia (Iraq) were great centres of learning.

In Europe, the Germanic peoples were skilled metalworkers. The village blacksmith was a central figure of their society because he made and mended all the iron tools.

◀ The Arabs were great astronomers. They invented the astrolabe, a device which measures the angle of a star in relation to the horizon, so they could navigate by measuring the altitude of stars and planets. At Baghdad there was an observatory and a 'House of Learning' where scholars translated ancient Greek works into Arabic. Arab astronomers drew star constellations as human figures. The one shown here is called Cepheus.

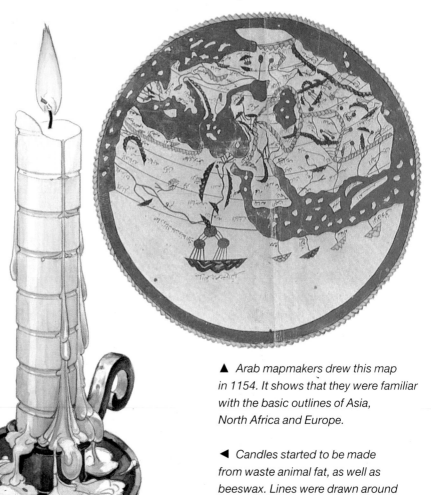

▲ Arab mapmakers drew this map in 1154. It shows that they were familiar with the basic outlines of Asia, North Africa and Europe.

◀ Candles started to be made from waste animal fat, as well as beeswax. Lines were drawn around them to make a simple clock.

751 The technique of paper-making spreads from China to the Muslim world.

762 Baghdad, a centre of learning, is founded.

c. 825 An Arab mathematician describes the Indian decimal system, later called the Hindu-Arabic numeral system.

c. 900 The Chinese develop porcelain.

971 Universities are established in the Arab world. One of the first is in Cairo, Egypt.

1000 Pottery starts to be made with moulds in Central and North America.

1100 Universities open in Christian Europe.

▶ *The Chinese mostly used fireworks in religious rituals. A scientist discovered gunpowder by accident when the potion he was mixing exploded, setting his beard on fire.*

◀ *This Chinese compass is made of magnetic stone. The figure on top always points south.*

▼ *Charcoal, which was used in metal smelting, was made from wood. Branches were piled up, then covered with earth, leaving an opening at the top. A fire was lit at the bottom and the wood dried out slowly, leaving charcoal behind.*

987 France: Hugh Capet is elected king (to 996) and founds the Capetian dynasty.

988 Russia: Vladimir of Kiev introduces the Christian Eastern Orthodox Church into his lands.

991 England: At the battle of Maldon, Byrhtnoth of Essex is defeated by Danish invaders. Later Ethelred II buys off the Danes with 10,000 pounds (in weight) of silver.

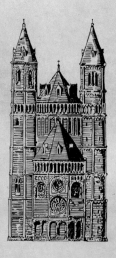

In about the 11th century Europe began a period of prosperity. This growth in wealth was marked by the construction of many impressive buildings, such as this huge Romanesque cathedral at Worms in Germany.

992 Ethelred makes a truce with Duke Richard I of Normandy. Boleslaw the Brave, son of Mieszko, becomes king of Poland. He rules until 1025.

993 Sweden: Olaf Skutkonung is the first Christian king. He rules until 1024.

994 England: The Danes under Sweyn Forkbeard and the Norwegians under Olaf Tryggvason sail up the River Thames and besiege London, until Ethelred buys them off.

995 Olaf Tryggvason returns to Norway, deposes Haakon the Great, and makes himself king. Japan: A literary and artistic golden age starts under the rule of Fujiwara Michinaga. It lasts until 1028.

996 France: Richard II becomes duke of Normandy until 1027. Hugh Capet's son, Robert, also known as Robert the Pious, becomes king of France (to 1031).

998 Asia: Mahmud, the Turkish ruler of Ghazni (to 1030), founds an empire in northern India and eastern Afghanistan.

The Capetians

In France the Carolingian dynasty was followed by that of the Capetians in 987. Capet was a nickname which had been given to the dynasty's founder because of the short cape he wore when he was lay (not a clergyman) abbot of St Martin de Tours. As Hugh, Duke of Francia, he was the most powerful vassal of Louis V, the last Carolingian king of France. Duke Charles of Lorraine claimed a right to the throne by descent from Carolingian monarchs, but Hugh schemed to have himself elected as king by seeking the support of wealthy, land-owning bishops.

Although Hugh Capet was king, his position was not very strong. From his capital in Paris, he ruled directly over a large part of northern France. In the rest of the country, however, some of his vassals were almost as powerful as he was. These included the dukes of Normandy, Burgundy and Aquitaine. Luckily for Hugh, no single one of them was strong enough to overthrow him

▲ *When Hugh Capet came to power, France was divided into large duchies. The most important of them were Normandy, Burgundy and Aquitaine.*

and they were all too jealous of each other to make an alliance against him.

Hugh Capet made sure the succession passed to his son by having him crowned as king of France while he was still alive. In this he was copying the Holy Roman emperors who had their sons crowned king of the Romans. This meant that no one could contest the throne. The practice continued for the next two centuries, helping to make France into a stable country. Later Capetian kings enlarged royal territory, increased the powers of the king and gave the country a strong central government.

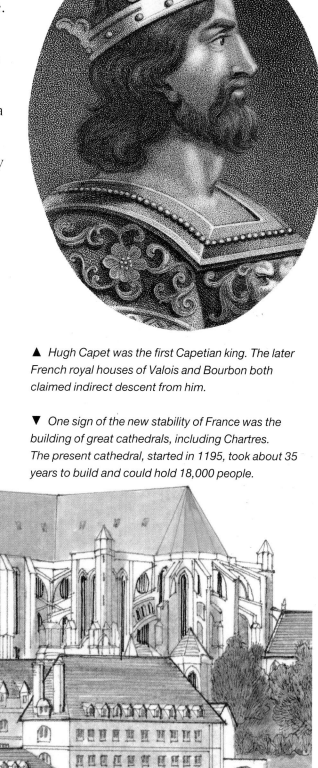

▲ Hugh Capet was the first Capetian king. The later French royal houses of Valois and Bourbon both claimed indirect descent from him.

▼ One sign of the new stability of France was the building of great cathedrals, including Chartres. The present cathedral, started in 1195, took about 35 years to build and could hold 18,000 people.

The Vikings

In the late 8th century, the Vikings began to venture from their homelands of Norway, Denmark and Sweden in search of treasure and better farmland. They made excellent wooden ships, lightweight and flat-bottomed, which could sail up rivers as well as on rough seas. They could also land on beaches and so could go to places where there were no harbours. At first their targets were monasteries, but later they attacked coastal towns. They sailed along the rivers Rhine, Seine and Loire to attack inland cities such as Paris and Cologne. Local rulers bought them off with large amounts of silver or gold.

Not all Vikings were raiders, however. Many were farmers looking for new land

▲ The Vikings were skilled metalworkers. This is a die, used for stamping an identifying pattern onto a metal sheet. It shows two legendary warriors about to attack a ferocious beast. The Vikings also made gold and silver jewellery, and swords and axes from iron.

▼ Viking warriors sailed in longships which often had a dragon's head at the front. Although the Vikings usually fought in small groups they were fearless fighters both at sea and on land. Viking ships had a keel, a long narrow piece of wood attached to the underside. This made their ships faster and easier to steer.

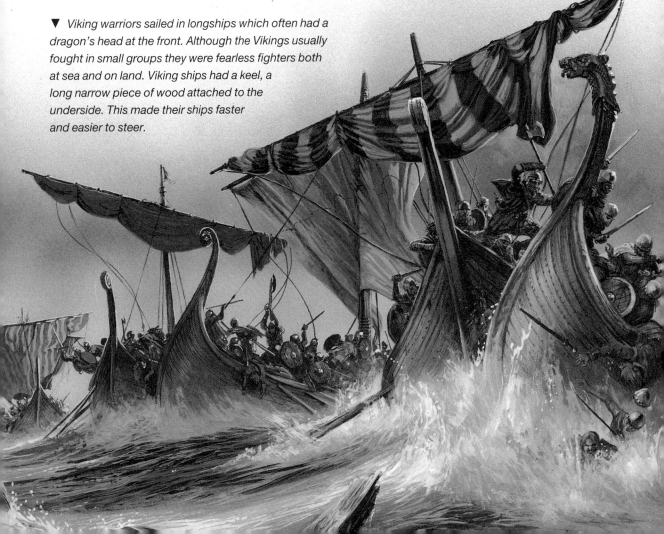

as there was not enough for everyone in their homelands. In Britain they settled mainly in northern and eastern England, northern Scotland, the Isle of Man and Ireland. In France they settled in Normandy which was given to their leader, Rollo, by the king of France in 911. Others settled in Iceland and some went on from there to Greenland and the east coast of North America. The Vikings often married local people. They adopted local languages, but added words of their own to them (our days of the week are named after the gods Tyr, Odin or Woden, Thor and Frigg). They wrote in runes, stick-like letters, which were carved on stone, wood or metal.

▲ A Viking man and woman in everyday clothes. These were practical, rather than fashionable. Their silver jewellery was sometimes cut up and used as money.

999 Africa: Bagauda becomes the first king of Kano (now in Nigeria). Europe: As the year 1000 approaches, people fear the Last Judgement and the end of the world will come. The Poles conquer Silesia.

The seven warriors depicted on the Lindisfarne stone, shown here, are thought to represent the Vikings who raided the monastery in 793.

1000 Hungary: Stephen I, later to be known as St Stephen, becomes the first king. He rules until 1038. North America: The Viking Bjarni Herjolfsson sights the coast of North America when he is blown off course in a storm. Denmark: At the battle of Svolder, Sweyn Forkbeard kills Olaf of Norway and annexes Norway. England: Ethelred II ravages Cumberland. China: The invention of gunpowder is perfected. Africa: The kingdom of Ghana reaches the height of its power. It controls Atlantic ports, as well as trade routes across the Sahara.

1002 England: King Ethelred marries Emma, sister of Duke Richard of Normandy. In the Massacre of St Brice's day, Ethelred orders all Danes in southern England to be killed.

1003 England: Sweyn Forkbeard, King of Denmark, lands to avenge the massacre. North America: Leif Ericsson, son of Eric the Red, journeys down the coast, possibly as far as Maryland, USA.

1007 England: Ethelred buys two years of peace from the Danes for 36,000 pounds (in weight) of silver.

1012 The Danes sack Canterbury, before being bought off for 48,000 pounds (in weight) of silver.

1013 Sweyn lands in England again and is made king. Ethelred flees to Normandy.

1014 Sweyn Forkbeard dies suddenly and the English recall Ethelred II from Normandy to be their king. Ireland: The king, Brian Boru, defeats the Vikings at the battle of Clontarf. He allows them to stay in Ireland, however, because they bring wealth to the country through their trading ports.

1015 England: Sweyn Forkbeard's son, Canute, now king of Denmark, invades and war between the Saxons and the Danes starts.

1016 England: Ethelred II dies. His son, Edmund Ironside, becomes king, but then agrees to share the country with Canute. Edmund rules Wessex, while Canute rules the north. When Edmund is assassinated, Canute becomes king of England. Olaf II becomes king of Norway.

1017 Canute divides England into four earldoms: Wessex, Mercia, Northumbria, and East Anglia.

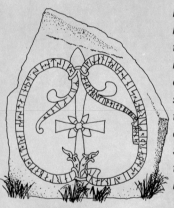

Runes, straight stick-like letters, were used by the Vikings to write inscriptions in wood or on stone. Many stones still stand and have taught historians a great deal. This one in Sweden commemorates the building of the road by which it stands.

1018 India: Mahmud of Ghazni pillages the sacred city of Muttra.

1019 To strengthen his claim to the English throne Canute marries Emma of Normandy, widow of Ethelred II.

1021 Islamic empire: Caliph al-Hakim declares himself divine and founds the Druse sect.

1024 Holy Roman Empire: Conrad II, becomes king of Germany and Holy Roman emperor until 1039.

1027 France: Robert the Devil is duke of Normandy. He rules until 1035.

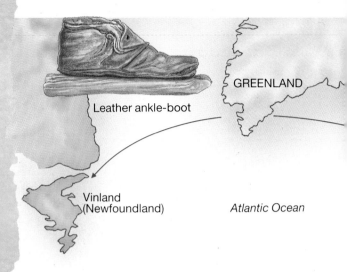

Leather ankle-boot

GREENLAND

Vinland
(Newfoundland)

Atlantic Ocean

The Vikings sailed across the Atlantic Ocean at a time when most people did not dare to sail out of sight of land. From Iceland they colonized Greenland around 985. At the same time Bjarni Herjolfsson saw the coast of North America when he was blown off course by a storm. He did not land there, but told people in Greenland of what he had seen. Leif Ericsson went in search of this new land, which he called Vinland, the Land of Grapes (the grapes were probably gooseberries or cranberries, used to make wine). The Vikings settled there briefly around 1003. Traces of settlement have been found in Newfoundland, Canada, and at Maine in the United States.

Swedish Vikings sailed east across the Baltic and into Russia (*see* pages 184–185). They were traders rather than settlers and set up trading posts at Novgorod and Kiev. From there they sailed down rivers to the Black Sea and Constantinople where they traded for goods from as far away as China. Some sailed into the Mediterranean and visited Jerusalem and Greece. Others sailed into the Mediterranean from the west and fought with the Arabs and the southern Europeans. Descendants of the Norman Vikings in France later colonized southern Italy and the island of Sicily.

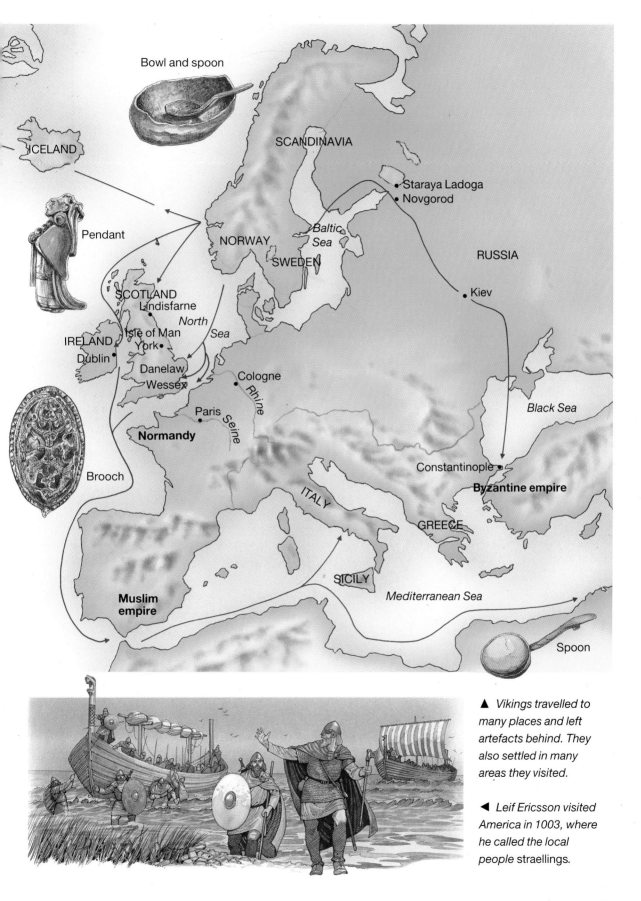

Bowl and spoon

ICELAND

Pendant

SCANDINAVIA

Staraya Ladoga
Novgorod

Baltic
Sea

NORWAY

SWEDEN

RUSSIA

SCOTLAND
Lindisfarne

Kiev

North

IRELAND

Isle of Man

Sea

York

Dublin

Danelaw

Wessex

Cologne

Rhine

Paris

Seine

Normandy

Black Sea

Brooch

Constantinople

Byzantine empire

ITALY

GREECE

SICILY

Mediterranean Sea

Muslim
empire

Spoon

▲ *Vikings travelled to
many places and left
artefacts behind. They
also settled in many
areas they visited.*

◄ *Leif Ericsson visited
America in 1003, where
he called the local
people straellings.*

Society and Government

In China all power was concentrated in the hands of the emperor. He could conscript people into his army or force them to work for him. Japan also had an emperor, but he spent a lot of his time studying religious matters while a regent ran his country for him.

In the Islamic empire, people were governed by Islamic Law. This included laws on food and drink, prayer and pilgrimages.

The Byzantine empire under Justinian based its laws on those of the old Roman empire. Further north and west, however, society was governed differently. The emergence of strong kings like Charlemagne led to the development of the feudal system. In contrast, the Vikings had no kings at all until the late 9th century. Instead, they were governed by *things*, which met to solve disputes and make new laws. Every freeman could vote. Those who refused to accept the law of the thing became outlaws. Many Viking laws were similar to Saxon laws. One law said a criminal had to pay compensation to his victim.

▲ Muslims travelled widely (part of their faith decreed that they had to make at least one pilgrimage to the Ka'aba in Mecca). Their travels helped to spread ideas, as well as trading goods. Not all societies approved of merchants, however. In China and Japan the poorest soldier was considered to be more important than a trader.

▲ Under the Vikings and Saxons, people were often tried by a jury of 12 men. Later, trial by fire or hot water became more common. The accused person had to walk barefoot across hot coals or (right) put his hand into boiling water. He was innocent if the burns healed.

◀ *A wall painting from the tomb of the Chinese princess Yung T'ai. Yung T'ai was forced to commit suicide at 17 for criticizing her grandmother, Empress Yu. In Chinese society, ancestors and parents were highly respected and children had to obey their parents, even when they became adults.*

▼ *In England, the Normans adopted many of the old laws. The lord of the manor dealt with small offences. The shire court was used for more serious crimes, or those involving property. This one, held in 1072, met to decide whether some lands belonged to the Bishop of Bayeux or to Canterbury Cathedral.*

WHEN IT HAPPENED

622 Islam attracts many poor people in Arabia because its teachings offer a fairer society.

858 Regents start to rule Japan for the emperor.

1086 By this date most land in England belongs to the Normans. The feudal system gives the nobility all the power.

1028 Norway: The Danes under Canute conquer the country. His son, Sweyn, becomes king of Norway. Byzantine empire: Zoë starts to rule the country in her own right. Arabia: Asma, the ruling queen of the Yemen, is succeeded by her daughter-in-law, Arwa, bypassing the sultan, al-Mukarram, with his consent.

1030 Norway: Olaf tries to regain the throne, but is killed at the battle of Stiklestad.

1031 France: Henry I rules until 1060.

1034 Scotland: Duncan is king (to 1040).

1035 Canute dies and his possessions are divided. His illegitimate son, Harold Harefoot, rules England as Harold I until 1040. Harthacanute becomes king of Denmark. France: William, the illegitimate son of Robert the Devil, becomes duke of Normandy.

1039 Holy Roman Empire: Henry III, also called Henry the Black, becomes emperor (to 1056).

The top border of the Bayeaux Tapestry is embroidered with many fantastic animal figures from mythology.

1040 England: Harthacanute becomes king. Scotland: Macbeth kills Duncan in battle and becomes king (to 1057).

1042 England: Harthacanute dies and is followed by Edward the Confessor, son of Ethelred II. Real power is in the hands of Earl Godwin of Wessex and his sons. Denmark: Magnus the Good, son of Olaf II, becomes king to 1047.

1046 Harald Hardrada becomes king of Norway.

1047 Canute's nephew, Sweyn II, becomes king of Denmark until 1076.

1051 England: Godwin is banished for opposing the king. He returns in 1052 with a fleet to win back his power.

1052 England: Edward the Confessor founds Westminster Abbey, near London.

England

In 978 Ethelred II became king of England. He ruled until 1016, but it was not a peaceful time. Armies of Danes and Norwegians kept attacking and Ethelred had to bribe them to go away. This made him unpopular with the people, who had to provide the money. In 1013, Sweyn Forkbeard, King of Denmark, landed in England and was proclaimed king. Ethelred fled to France.

Ethelred returned the next year when Sweyn died, but in 1015 Sweyn's son, Canute, came to England and in 1016 he became its king. He ruled until his death in 1035, when he was succeeded by his son, Harthacanute. When he died in 1042, Edward the Confessor, son of Ethelred II, was chosen as king of England. He had been brought up in Normandy and was very religious. He relied heavily on Godwin, Earl of

▼ *A panel from the Bayeux Tapestry showing the deathbed of Edward the Confessor when he is said to have named Harold as his successor even though he had already promised William the throne of England.*

CANUTE

c. **994** Born.
1016 Invades England and becomes king.
1018 Becomes king of Denmark.
1019 Marries Emma, Ethelred's widow.
1028 Invades Norway, makes his son king.
1035 Dies.

EDWARD

c. **1002** Born, son of Ethelred II.
1042 Becomes king with the support of Earl Godwin of Wessex. Known for his piety he founds Westminster Abbey, but he is a weak ruler.
1066 Dies.

▲ *Canute's kingdom included Denmark, England and Norway, along with Danish lands in southern Sweden.*

▼ *The battle of Hastings took place just 19 days after Harold had defeated Harald Hardrada at Stamford Bridge. Harold had marched south and raised a fresh army, but he was killed and his troops were defeated.*

Wessex, and Godwin's son, Harold, to govern the country for him.

When Edward died without an heir in 1066, Harold Godwinsson was chosen to replace him. Harald Hardrada, King of Norway, also claimed the throne and attacked England, but Harold defeated him near York. Three days later a Norman army invaded England and Harold was defeated in the battle of Hastings by William, Duke of Normandy.

The Feudal System

Feudalism was a system under which people held land in exchange for services, rather than for rent. It developed in the 8th century under the Franks and gradually spread across western Europe. William the Conqueror brought it to England when he became William I. He believed that all the land in the country belonged to him. To help him raise money and have an army

▶ *Early medieval society was strictly divided and everyone knew his or her place. At the top was the king who granted land to barons and to the church. The barons built castles for defence **1** and lived in large manor houses **2**. In return for military service they granted land to knights **3**. By the side of the manor house were farm buildings **4** and the house of the bailiff **5** who managed the estate. The farm work was done by villeins and brodars who, to protect their lord's privacy, lived in the village **6**.*

when he needed one, he allowed his barons to hold some of this land. In exchange for these estates, they paid him taxes and provided him with knights to help him fight his enemies.

In turn, the barons allowed their knights to hold some of their land. In exchange for these manors, each knight had to give the baron 40 days' military service each year. For this he had to be armed and on horseback and also have a certain number of soldiers with him.

Each knight allowed people known as *villeins* to hold land from him. They were the largest group in society at this time. They usually lived in villages near the manor house and farmed around 12 hectares of land each. They had to work two or three days a week for the lord of the manor. They also had to give him some of their crops or an equal amount in money. There were also *brodars* who had about two hectares of land. A village was largely self-supporting and people rarely travelled beyond its boundaries.

1053 England: Earl Godwin dies. His son Harold succeeds him as earl of Wessex.

1054 The final break comes between the Byzantine empire and the Roman Church; the Eastern Orthodox Church becomes completely independent. West Africa: Abdallah ben Yassim begins the Muslim conquest.

1055 England: Harold Godwinsson's brother, Tostig, becomes earl of Northumbria.

Hunting was a popular sport for both noblemen and noblewomen.

1056 Holy Roman Empire: Henry IV is emperor (to 1106). His mother is regent.

1057 Scotland: Duncan's son, Malcolm, defeats and kills Macbeth. Macbeth's stepson, Lulach, becomes king for a year.

1058 Scotland: Malcolm (Canmore) becomes king after killing Lulach in battle (until 1093). Poland: Boleslaw the Bold becomes king and conquers Upper Slovakia.

1060 France: Philip I is king (to 1108).

1061 Scotland: Malcolm invades Northumbria. North Africa: The Muslim Almoravid dynasty is founded and later conquers Spain.

1062 North Africa: Yusuf ben Tashfin founds Marrakesh, in Morocco.

1063 England: Harold and his brother Tostig subdue Wales. Africa: The kingdom of Ghana under Tunka Manin has an army of 200,000.

1064 France: Harold Godwinsson is shipwrecked in Normandy and is possibly tricked into swearing an oath to support William of Normandy's claim to England.

The Normans

William the Conqueror was crowned William I of England on Christmas Day 1066. In Normandy, however, he was still only a duke and a vassal of the king of France. At first many people in the north and east of England protested against his rule. He put down these rebellions brutally, taking the land and giving it to his followers. To keep the peace, he introduced the feudal system (*see* pages 68–69). He gave much land to the church and replaced most of the English bishops with French ones. He also encouraged traders and craftsmen from France to settle in England.

In William's reign, the landscape of England and Wales started to change. He

▶ *William I was followed by two of his sons. William II ruled from 1087 to 1100 and Henry I from 1100 to 1135. They established firm Norman rule, but it collapsed under the next king, Stephen.*

▼ *The Normans enjoyed hunting and created many areas known as forests. These did not all have trees. Instead, they were places where animals were kept to be hunted by rich people. It was forbidden for anyone to enter a royal forest with bow and arrows or dogs, without a special warrant.*

▲ *The connection between England and Normandy gave the English monarch control of land in France.*

▼ *In 1085 William ordered a survey of England to find out who owned the land, who lived there, how much it was worth and what taxes he could expect. The survey was written up in the* Domesday Book, *shown here.*

and many of his followers built large castles and towns grew up around them. The old churches were replaced by bigger ones and the great cathedrals such as Winchester and Durham were begun. Monks and nuns from France set up large monasteries and convents in the countryside and attracted new followers from the local populations. French became the language of the nobility.

Although Norman rule was harsh, it brought advantages: castles provided refuges for local people when attacked; the civil service (the work of running the country) was started; and the first survey of English land was carried out.

1066 England: Edward the Confessor dies on 5 January. Although he was married, he has no children. Harold Godwinsson claims the throne and is crowned as King Harold II of England on 6 January. Harold's brother, Tostig, joins forces with Harald Hardrada of Norway to invade England in September. Harold's army defeats and kills them both at the battle of Stamford Bridge. While Harold and his army are in the north, William of Normandy lands on the south coast of England. Harold marches south and meets William's army at the battle of Hastings just 19 days after the battle of Stamford Bridge. Harold is killed and his army defeated. William declares himself king of England and is crowned in Westminster Abbey on Christmas Day.

Manuscripts telling stories about courtly love and romance between lords and ladies were very popular in Norman England.

1067 England: Work starts on building the Tower of London. Italy: Monte Cassino monastery is rebuilt.

1068 England: The Norman conquest continues until 1069. William subdues the north of England by laying it waste. This is known as the 'Harrying of the North'. China: Shen Tsung is emperor (to 1085). His minister Wang Anshi carries out some radical reforms.

1069 Egypt: A famine there lasts until 1072.

1070 England: Hereward the Wake begins a Saxon revolt in the Fens, East Anglia.

Trade

After the collapse of the Roman empire, trade became more difficult in Europe. Roman roads fell into disrepair and traders were at the mercy of robbers. Most goods went by sea if possible.

From the East, merchants travelled along the Silk Road and across the Sahara Desert. Important commodities included salt and spices. The greatest traders were the Vikings and the Arabs. They traded with each other in Baghdad and Constantinople, where furs, walrus ivory and slaves were exchanged for silk, spices and silver.

▲ *This Viking coin was made in the 9th century. Coins were valued for the silver or gold they contained.*

◄ *A Tang model of an Armenian trader. The Chinese preferred to let foreigners handle their trade.*

▼ *The Vikings used sturdy ships called* knarrs *to transport their goods down the rivers of Russia to the markets of Constantinople.*

▶ This statue of Buddha was found at Helgo in Sweden. It was buried in about the 8th century, and shows that even before the Viking age, Swedish traders had found their way East.

▲ As populations expanded, more people went to live in the towns. Some became weavers, but they did not own their own sheep. They bought wool from merchants who travelled around from farm to farm, buying up any wool the farmers did not need. Soon nearly all wool was sent to the towns.

WHEN IT HAPPENED

c. **501** In South America the powerful Tiahuanaco empire controls the trade of drugs used in religious ceremonies.

800 The kingdom of Ghana starts to trade in gold and salt and grow rich.

841 The Vikings build a settlement at Dublin in Ireland. It attracts both merchants and craftsmen.

850 Vikings from Sweden start to visit Russia. Soon after this date, they set up trading posts and make their way down the rivers in Russia to Constantinople.

1071 The East African ports of Kilwa and Gedi send ambassadors to China in order to set up trading links.

▲ Arab traders who crossed the deserts of Asia and North Africa carried their goods on camels. They could travel 320 kilometres in a week. If a well or oasis was dry, however, they might all die.

The Seljuk Empire

Nomadic Turks from the steppes of central Asia founded their first kingdom in Afghanistan in the late 10th century. As it expanded, it attracted more tribes of Turks into the area. In the late 900s, a tribal chief called Seljuk and his followers settled around the oasis of Merv, near Bokhara in Uzbekistan. There they were ruled by the Ghaznavid Turks from Afghanistan. In 1037, however, the Seljuks occupied Merv and in 1040 they defeated the Ghaznavids. After that, the Seljuks started to build up their own empire.

Under the leadership of Toghril Beg (990-1063), the Seljuks swept through present-day Iran and Iraq to conquer Baghdad in 1055. Toghril Beg was expelled for a short time by an uprising, but came back to power. When he died his nephew, Alp Arslan, took power.

Alp Arslan continued to expand the

▲ The Seljuks made great conquests between 1037 and 1092. After the death of Malik Shah the empire started to split into separate countries.

▼ Like most people from the steppes of Central Asia, the Seljuks were great horsemen. They used stirrups and could fire arrows from horseback very accurately. This picture shows them beating the Byzantines at Manzikert. This victory gave the Seljuks control of Anatolia, which was later part of the Ottoman empire.

THE LION HERO

The Seljuk leader Alp Arslan (whose name literally means the Lion Hero) was sultan from 1063 to 1072. He was a skillful and brave commander who devoted his energies to extending the Seljuk empire. His victory at Manzikert opened up Anatolia to the Muslims. He was killed in a struggle with a prisoner while fighting in Persia. His son later conquered Syria and Palestine.

▲ *The Seljuks became Muslims around 970. This minaret at the Jami Mosque in Simnan, built around the time of the conquest of present day Iran, has typical Seljuk patterns in its elaborate brickwork.*

Seljuk empire. In 1064 he captured the capital of Armenia and raided Constantinople. In 1071 the Byzantine emperor decided to fight back. While Alp Arslan was in Syria, the Byzantine army marched into Armenia from the west. Alp Arslan heard of this and marched in from the south. The armies fought at Manzikert. The Seljuks won because they pretended to be defeated and ran away. When the Byzantines went after them, they turned around and defeated the Byzantine army heavily. The Seljuks captured the Byzantine emperor and held him to ransom. This victory laid the foundation for what later became the Ottoman empire.

The Seljuk empire reached its greatest power under the rule of Alp Arslan's son, Malik Shah (1072-1092). He was a patron of science and the arts and built fine mosques in his capital, Isfahan.

1071 Anatolia: At the battle of Manzikert, the Seljuk leader Alp Arslan defeats the Byzantine empire's army and conquers most of Anatolia.

1072 Mediterranean: Normans invade Sicily. By 1091 they have conquered the whole island. England: William I invades Scotland; in East Anglia Hereward the Wake submits. Spain: Alfonso VI is king of Castile.

1073 Gregory VII becomes pope until 1085.

1075 A dispute starts between the pope and the Holy Roman emperor over who should appoint bishops. Near East: The Seljuk leader Malik Shah conquers Syria and Palestine.

1076 Holy Roman Empire: At the Synod of Worms, the bishops depose Pope Gregory. Pope Gregory then excommunicates Emperor Henry IV.

This bronze deer was made as a fountain in Muslim Spain. The water was drawn up through the legs and body and came out of the mouth.

1077 Holy Roman Empire: The dispute between the emperor and the pope leads to civil war starting in the empire. Henry, frightened of losing his throne, does penance to Pope Gregory at Canossa. Africa: In Ghana the Almoravid dynasty takes control.

1080 Denmark: Canute IV rules (to 1086). Holy Roman Empire: Henry IV is again excommunicated and declared deposed by Pope Gregory. The civil war ends.

1081 Alexius I Comnenus becomes the Byzantine emperor (to 1118).

1083 The Holy Roman emperor Henry IV attacks Rome.

1084 Robert Guiscard, Duke of Apulia, forces Henry IV to retreat to Germany.

1085 Spain: Alfonso VI captures Toledo from the Moors.

1086 The Danish threat to England ends when Canute IV of Denmark is assassinated. England: The *Domesday Book* is completed and the feudal system established.

1087 England: William I dies, leaving Normandy to his oldest son, Robert, and England to his second son, William Rufus. To his third son, Henry, he leaves some money.

1088 Urban II becomes pope (to 1099).

1090 Persia: The Assassin sect is founded by Hasan ibn al-Sabbah, the first 'Old Man of the Mountain'.

1093 Scotland: Donald Bane becomes king, after the death of his brother, Malcolm III, in battle against the English.

During the Song dynasty, Chinese emperors had factories built to make porcelain especially for their palaces.

1096 The First Crusade begins, after Pope Urban II appeals for volunteers to free the Christian holy places in Palestine from the Muslims or Saracens.

1097 Scotland: Malcolm's second son, Edgar, becomes king of Scotland after William II of England helps him to defeat Donald Bane.

1098 France: The first Cistercian monastery is founded at Citeaux. The Crusaders defeat the Muslims at Antioch.

1099 Palestine: The Crusaders capture Jerusalem and elect Godfrey of Bouillon as its king.

1100 England: Henry, youngest son of William I, becomes king after the assassination of William II. Italy: Bologna University is founded. Palestine: Some parts are ruled by Crusaders; Baldwin of Bouillon is count of Edessa, Raymond of Toulouse is count of Tripoli, and Bohemund of Otranto is prince of Antioch.

The Song Dynasty

After the fall of the Tang dynasty in 907, five emperors in 53 years tried to reunite China and start new dynasties. None of them succeeded until the first Song emperor who came to the throne in 960. Although the country was finally reunited the Chinese empire was smaller than it had been in the past. In the north-west was Tibet and in the north-east was Lao, to whom the Song paid a tribute in silk. The first Song emperor worked hard to bring peace to his country. Agriculture expanded and the population grew rapidly. By the end of the Song period there were probably around 100 million people living in China.

In 1068 the prime minister, Wang Anshi, tried to reform the government of China. He made the tax system simpler and cut the huge army down to a reasonably sized fighting force. Although these cuts saved money, they also made it easier for other peoples to invade China, especially from the north.

▲ *The Song dynasty was split into two parts. The first is the Northern Song, with its capital at Kaifeng. Later the Southern Song ruled only the south of the empire.*

◀ *This picture is painted with ink on silk. At this time the Chinese often painted natural objects such as animals, flowers or landscapes, but they did not always make them look realistic.*

The Song emperors managed to keep defeating the invaders until 1126. In that year the emperor and his family were captured and the Song lost control of the north. Only one son escaped because he was away from home. He moved to Hangzhou and made it the capital of a new empire, known as the Southern Song. This lasted until 1279 when it was overrun by the Mongols under Kublai Khan.

In spite of the threat of invasions, the arts flourished in the Song dynasty. Pictures were painted on silk and paper. Fine porcelain was produced and exported to places such as India and the east coast of Africa. Many poems were written and professional storytellers wandered round the countryside, performing in exchange for money.

▶ *This wine vessel in a lotus shaped warmer is one of the many beautiful, fine porcelain objects which were produced during the Song dynasty.*

LILY FEET

The Chinese thought women should have tiny feet, called lily feet. The feet were tightly bound from birth to stop them growing normally. As a result, most rich women could hardly walk.

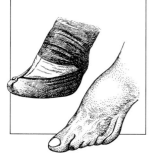

INVENTIONS

Chinese technology was more advanced than that of the west. Under the Song they made firearms and bombs. They built ships, used a compass and made clocks. In medicine, they understood how vaccination worked. They made the best silk in the world and their pottery was so fine that today we call porcelain 'china'.

War and Weapons

Weapons became more effective with the introduction of iron. Swords and knives were made from it, as were the heads of battleaxes and spears. In turn, this meant that soldiers needed better protection. At first they used wooden shields covered in leather. Later chain mail was worn. It was expensive to make, so many wore a thick leather breastplate instead.

Early battles in this period were fought on foot. Later, when stirrups were introduced into Europe, horses became more important in war.

In Europe, armies were still quite small, while in China and Arabia they numbered thousands.

▼ *Stirrups, introduced into Europe in the 8th century, gave horsemen a more secure seat in battle.*

▲ *At the battle of Hastings the English fought on foot with axes and spears. Although they were protected behind a wall of shields, they could not match the Normans, who fought on horseback.*

WHEN IT HAPPENED
553 The Franks are defeated and massacred at the battle of Casilinum, near Capua, in Italy.
636 The Arabs defeat the Byzantines at Yarmuk.
732 Charles Martel defeats the Moors at Poitiers.
793 The Vikings raid the monastery of Lindisfarne off the north-east coast of England.
1066 King Harold of England defeats King Harald of Norway at the battle of Stamford Bridge. Then Harold is defeated by William, Duke of Normandy at the battle of Hastings.
1071 The Seljuk Turks defeat the Byzantines at Manzikert and conquer most of Anatolia.

◄ *Viking soldiers often carried a spear in battle. It was made of ash wood and had an iron head. These were thrown at the enemy and gathered up after the battle.*

► *Viking raiders went in search of treasure and slaves, often travelling in small numbers. Their raids were usually successful because they came to the towns and villages without warning.*

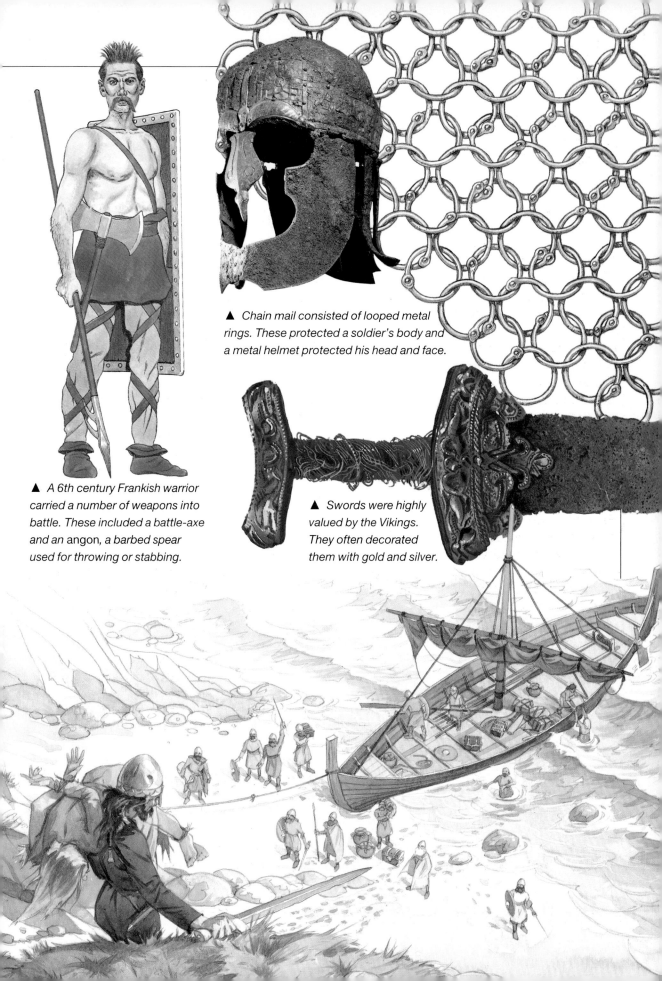

▲ Chain mail consisted of looped metal rings. These protected a soldier's body and a metal helmet protected his head and face.

▲ A 6th century Frankish warrior carried a number of weapons into battle. These included a battle-axe and an angon, a barbed spear used for throwing or stabbing.

▲ Swords were highly valued by the Vikings. They often decorated them with gold and silver.

New Zealand

People from the Polynesian Islands in the Pacific probably first reached New Zealand by canoe around 1000. They settled mainly on the North Island which was much bigger and cooler than their homelands. It had plants, birds and animals that were unlike those the Polynesians were used to. At first the Maori culture was based on hunting. One favourite food was a flightless bird called the moa. When this had been hunted to extinction, the Maoris turned to farming to provide food. They lived in wooden houses in large, fortified villages and their main crops were sweet potatoes and fern rhizomes. They were fierce warriors and could use either male or female lines of descent to claim rights to land. Their religion was based on taboos which meant that certain objects, persons and places were sacred and forbidden to certain members of the group.

▼ As well as being farmers and warriors, the Maoris were also skilled woodcarvers and decorated their houses with complicated designs. They had no metal tools and so used stone for axes to cut wood.

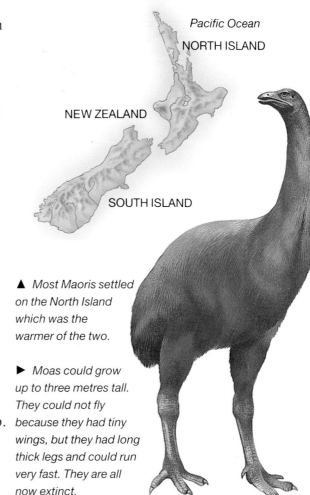

Pacific Ocean

NORTH ISLAND

NEW ZEALAND

SOUTH ISLAND

▲ Most Maoris settled on the North Island which was the warmer of the two.

▶ Moas could grow up to three metres tall. They could not fly because they had tiny wings, but they had long thick legs and could run very fast. They are all now extinct.

Index

This index has been designed to help you find easily the information you are looking for. Page numbers in *italic* type (slanting) refer to pages on which there are illustrations.